THE PELICAN SHAKESPEARE
GENERAL EDITORS

STEPHEN ORGEL
A. R. BRAUNMULLER

Romeo and Juliet

Spranger Barry and Isabella Nossiter, 1753

William Shakespeare

—

Romeo and Juliet

EDITED BY PETER HOLLAND

PENGUIN BOOKS

PENGUIN BOOKS

Published by the Penguin Group
Penguin Putnam Inc., 375 Hudson Street,
New York, New York 10014, U.S.A.
Penguin Books Ltd, 27 Wrights Lane,
London W8 5TZ, England
Penguin Books Australia Ltd, Ringwood,
Victoria, Australia
Penguin Books Canada Ltd, 10 Alcorn Avenue,
Toronto, Ontario, Canada M4V 3B2
Penguin Books (N.Z.) Ltd, 182–190 Wairau Road,
Auckland 10, New Zealand

Penguin Books Ltd, Registered Offices:
Harmondsworth, Middlesex, England

The Tragedy of Romeo and Juliet edited by John E. Hankins
published in the United States of America in Penguin Books 1960
Revised edition published 1970
This new edition edited by Peter Holland published 2000

1   3   5   7   9   10   8   6   4   2

Copyright © Penguin Books Inc., 1960, 1970
Copyright © Penguin Putnam Inc., 2000
All rights reserved

ISBN 0-14-07.1484-7

Printed in the United States of America
Set in Garamond
Designed by Virginia Norey

Contents

Publisher's Note

IT IS ALMOST half a century since the first volumes of the Pelican Shakespeare appeared under the general editorship of Alfred Harbage. The fact that a new edition, rather than simply a revision, has been undertaken reflects the profound changes textual and critical studies of Shakespeare have undergone in the past twenty years. For the new Pelican series, the texts of the plays and poems have been thoroughly revised in accordance with recent scholarship, and in some cases have been entirely reedited. New introductions and notes have been provided in all the volumes. But the new Shakespeare is also designed as a successor to the original series; the previous editions have been taken into account, and the advice of the previous editors has been solicited where it was feasible to do so.

Certain textual features of the new Pelican Shakespeare should be particularly noted. All lines are numbered that contain a word, phrase, or allusion explained in the glossarial notes. In addition, for convenience, every tenth line is also numbered, in italics when no annotation is indicated. The intrusive and often inaccurate place headings inserted by early editors are omitted (as is becoming standard practice), but for the convenience of those who miss them, an indication of locale now appears as the first item in the annotation of each scene.

In the interest of both elegance and utility, each speech prefix is set in a separate line when the speaker's lines are in verse, except when those words form the second half of a verse line. Thus the verse form of the speech is kept visually intact. What is printed as verse and what is printed as prose has, in general, the authority of the original texts. Departures from the original texts in this regard have only the authority of editorial tradition and the judgment of the Pelican editors; and, in a few instances, are admittedly arbitrary.

The Theatrical World

ECONOMIC REALITIES determined the theatrical world in which Shakespeare's plays were written, performed, and received. For centuries in England, the primary theatrical tradition was nonprofessional. Craft guilds (or "mysteries") provided religious drama – mystery plays – as part of the celebration of religious and civic festivals, and schools and universities staged classical and neoclassical drama in both Latin and English as part of their curricula. In these forms, drama was established and socially acceptable. Professional theater, in contrast, existed on the margins of society. The acting companies were itinerant; playhouses could be any available space – the great halls of the aristocracy, town squares, civic halls, inn yards, fair booths, or open fields – and income was sporadic, dependent on the passing of the hat or on the bounty of local patrons. The actors, moreover, were considered little better than vagabonds, constantly in danger of arrest or expulsion.

In the late 1560s and 1570s, however, English professional theater began to gain respectability. Wealthy aristocrats fond of drama – the Lord Admiral, for example, or the Lord Chamberlain – took acting companies under their protection so that the players technically became members of their households and were no longer subject to arrest as homeless or masterless men. Permanent theaters were first built at this time as well, allowing the companies to control and charge for entry to their performances.

Shakespeare's livelihood, and the stunning artistic explosion in which he participated, depended on pragmatic and architectural effort. Professional theater requires ways to restrict access to its offerings; if it does not, and admission fees cannot be charged, the actors do not get paid, the costumes go to a pawnbroker, and there is no such thing as a professional, ongoing theatrical tradition. The answer to that economic need arrived in the late 1560s and 1570s with the creation of the so-called public or amphitheater playhouse. Recent discoveries indicate that the precursor of the Globe playhouse in London (where Shakespeare's mature plays were presented) and the Rose theater (which presented Christopher Marlowe's plays and some of Shakespeare's earliest ones) was the Red Lion theater of 1567. Archaeological studies of the foundations of the Rose and Globe theaters have revealed that the open-air theater of the 1590s and later was probably a polygonal building with fourteen to twenty or twenty-four sides, multistoried, from 75 to 100 feet in diameter, with a raised, partly covered "thrust" stage that projected into a group of standing patrons, or "groundlings," and a covered gallery, seating up to 2,500 or more (very crowded) spectators.

These theaters might have been about half full on any given day, though the audiences were larger on holidays or when a play was advertised, as old and new were, through printed playbills posted around London. The metropolitan area's late-Tudor, early-Stuart population (circa 1590–1620) has been estimated at about 150,000 to 250,000. It has been supposed that in the mid-1590s there were about 15,000 spectators per week at the public theaters; thus, as many as 10 percent of the local population went to the theater regularly. Consequently, the theaters' repertories – the plays available for this experienced and frequent audience – had to change often: in the month between September 15 and October 15, 1595, for instance, the Lord Admiral's Men performed twenty-eight times in eighteen different plays.

Since natural light illuminated the amphitheaters' stages, performances began between noon and two o'clock and ran without a break for two or three hours. They often concluded with a jig, a fencing display, or some other nondramatic exhibition. Weather conditions determined the season for the amphitheaters: plays were performed every day (including Sundays, sometimes, to clerical dismay) except during Lent – the forty days before Easter – or periods of plague, or sometimes during the summer months when law courts were not in session and the most affluent members of the audience were not in London.

To a modern theatergoer, an amphitheater stage like that of the Rose or Globe would appear an unfamiliar mixture of plainness and elaborate decoration. Much of the structure was carved or painted, sometimes to imitate marble; elsewhere, as under the canopy projecting over the stage, to represent the stars and the zodiac. Appropriate painted canvas pictures (of Jerusalem, for example, if the play was set in that city) were apparently hung on the wall behind the acting area, and tragedies were accompanied by black hangings, presumably something like crepe festoons or bunting. Although these theaters did not employ what we would call scenery, early modern spectators saw numerous large props, such as the "bar" at which a prisoner stood during a trial, the "mossy bank" where lovers reclined, an arbor for amorous conversation, a chariot, gallows, tables, trees, beds, thrones, writing desks, and so forth. Audiences might learn a scene's location from a sign (reading "Athens," for example) carried across the stage (as in Bertolt Brecht's twentieth-century productions). Equally captivating (and equally irritating to the theater's enemies) were the rich costumes and personal props the actors used: the most valuable items in the surviving theatrical inventories are the swords, gowns, robes, crowns, and other items worn or carried by the performers.

Magic appealed to Shakespeare's audiences as much as it does to us today, and the theater exploited many deceptive and spectacular devices. A winch in the loft above the stage, called "the heavens," could lower and raise actors playing gods, goddesses, and other supernatural figures to and from the main acting area, just as one or more trap-doors permitted entrances and exits to and from the area, called "hell," beneath the stage. Actors wore elementary makeup such as wigs, false beards, and face paint, and they employed pig's bladders filled with animal blood to make wounds seem more real. They had rudimentary but effective ways of pretending to behead or hang a person. Supernumeraries (stagehands or actors not needed in a particular scene) could make thunder sounds (by shaking a metal sheet or rolling an iron ball down a chute) and show lightning (by blowing inflammable resin through tubes into a flame). Elaborate fireworks enhanced the effects of dragons flying through the air or imitated such celestial phenomena as comets, shooting stars, and multiple suns. Horses' hoofbeats, bells (located perhaps in the tower above the stage), trumpets and drums, clocks, cannon shots and gunshots, and the like were common sound effects. And the music of viols, cornets, oboes, and recorders was a regular feature of theatrical performances.

For two relatively brief spans, from the late 1570s to 1590 and from 1599 to 1614, the amphitheaters competed with the so-called private, or indoor, theaters, which originated as, or later represented themselves as, educational institutions training boys as singers for church services and court performances. These indoor theaters had two features that were distinct from the amphitheaters': their personnel and their playing spaces. The amphitheaters' adult companies included both adult men, who played the male roles, and boys, who played the female roles; the private, or indoor, theater companies, on the other hand, were entirely composed of boys aged about 8 to 16, who were, or could pretend to be, candidates for singers in a church or a royal boys' choir. (Until 1660, professional theatrical companies included no women.) The playing space would appear much more familiar to modern audiences than the long-vanished amphitheaters; the later indoor theaters were, in fact, the ancestors of the typical modern theater. They were enclosed spaces, usually rectangular, with the stage filling one end of the rectangle and the audience arrayed in seats or benches across (and sometimes lining) the building's longer axis. These spaces staged plays less frequently than the public theaters (perhaps only once a week) and held far fewer spectators than the amphitheaters: about 200 to 600, as opposed to 2,500 or more. Fewer patrons mean a smaller gross income, unless each pays more. Not surprisingly, then, private theaters charged higher prices than the amphitheaters, probably sixpence, as opposed to a penny for the cheapest entry.

Protected from the weather, the indoor theaters presented plays later in the day than the amphitheaters, and used artificial illumination – candles in sconces or candelabra. But candles melt, and need replacing, snuffing, and trimming, and these practical requirements may have been part of the reason the indoor theaters introduced breaks in the performance, the intermission so dear to the heart of theatergoers and to the pocketbooks of theater concessionaires ever since. Whether motivated by the need to tend to the candles or by the entrepreneurs' wishing to sell oranges and liquor, or both, the indoor theaters eventually established the modern convention of the noncontinuous performance. In the early modern "private" theater, musical performances apparently filled the intermissions, which in Stuart theater jargon seem to have been called "acts."

At the end of the first decade of the seventeenth century, the distinction between public amphitheaters and private indoor companies ceased. For various cultural, political, and economic reasons, individual companies gained control of both the public, open-air theaters and the indoor ones, and companies mixing adult men and boys took over the formerly "private" theaters. Despite the death of the boys' companies and of their highly innovative theaters (for which such luminous playwrights as Ben Jonson, George Chapman, and John Marston wrote), their playing spaces and conventions had an immense impact on subsequent plays: not merely for the intervals (which stressed the artistic and architectonic importance of "acts"), but also because they introduced political and social satire as a popular dramatic ingredient, even in tragedy, and a wider range of actorly effects, encouraged by their more intimate playing spaces.

Even the briefest sketch of the Shakespearean theatrical world would be incomplete without some comment on the social and cultural dimensions of theaters and playing in the period. In an intensely hierarchical and status-conscious society, professional actors and their ventures had hardly any respectability; as we have indicated, to protect themselves against laws designed to curb vagabondage and the increase of masterless men, actors resorted to the near-fiction that they were the servants of noble masters, and wore their distinctive livery. Hence the company for which Shakespeare wrote in the 1590s called itself the Lord Chamberlain's Men and pretended that the public, money-getting performances were in fact rehearsals for private performances before that high court official. From 1598, the Privy Council had licensed theatrical companies, and after 1603, with the accession of King James I, the companies gained explicit royal protection, just as the Queen's Men had for a time under Queen Elizabeth. The Chamberlain's Men became the King's Men, and the other companies were patronized by the other members of the royal family.

These designations were legal fictions that half-concealed an important economic and social development, the evolution away from the theater's organization on the model of the guild, a self-regulating confraternity of individual artisans, into a proto-capitalist organization. Shakespeare's company became a joint-stock company, where persons who supplied capital and, in some cases, such as Shakespeare's, capital and talent, employed themselves and others in earning a return on that capital. This development meant that actors and theater companies were outside both the traditional guild structures, which required some form of civic or royal charter, and the feudal household organization of master-and-servant. This anomalous, maverick social and economic condition made theater companies practically unruly and potentially even dangerous; consequently, numerous official bodies – including the London metropolitan and ecclesiastical authorities as well as, occasionally, the royal court itself – tried, without much success, to control and even to disband them.

Public officials had good reason to want to close the theaters: they were attractive nuisances – they drew often riotous crowds, they were always noisy, and they could be politically offensive and socially insubordinate. Until the Civil War, however, anti-theatrical forces failed to shut down professional theater, for many reasons – limited surveillance and few police powers, tensions or outright hostilities among the agencies that sought to check or channel theatrical activity, and lack of clear policies for control. Another reason must have been the theaters' undeniable popularity. Curtailing any activity enjoyed by such a substantial percentage of the population was difficult, as various Roman emperors attempting to limit circuses had learned, and the Tudor-Stuart audience was not merely large, it was socially diverse and included women. The prevalence of public entertainment in this period has been underestimated. In fact, fairs, holidays, games, sporting events, the equivalent of modern parades, freak shows, and street exhibitions all abounded, but the theater was the most widely and frequently available entertainment to which people of every class had access. That fact helps account both for its quantity and for the fear and anger it aroused.

WILLIAM SHAKESPEARE OF
STRATFORD-UPON-AVON, GENTLEMAN

Many people have said that we know very little about William Shakespeare's life – pinheads and postcards are often mentioned as appropriately tiny surfaces on which to record the available information. More imaginatively and perhaps more correctly, Ralph Waldo Emerson wrote, "Shakespeare is the only biographer of Shakespeare. . . . So far from Shakespeare's being the least known, he is the one person in all modern history fully known to us."

In fact, we know more about Shakespeare's life than we do about almost any other English writer's of his era. His last will and testament (dated March 25, 1616) survives, as do numerous legal contracts and court documents involving Shakespeare as principal or witness, and parish records in Stratford and London. Shakespeare appears quite often in official records of King James's royal court, and of course Shakespeare's name appears on numerous title pages and in the written and recorded words of his literary contemporaries Robert Greene, Henry Chettle, Francis Meres, John Davies of Hereford, Ben Jonson, and many others. Indeed, if we make due allowance for the bloating of modern, run-of-the-mill bureaucratic records, more information has survived over the past four hundred years about William Shakespeare of Stratford-upon-Avon, Warwickshire, than is likely to survive in the next four hundred years about any reader of these words.

What we do not have are entire categories of information – Shakespeare's private letters or diaries, drafts and revisions of poems and plays, critical prefaces or essays, commendatory verse for other writers' works, or instructions guiding his fellow actors in their performances, for instance – that we imagine would help us understand and appreciate his surviving writings. For all we know, many such data never existed as written records. Many literary and theatrical critics, not knowing what might once have existed, more or less cheerfully accept the situation; some even make a theoretical virtue of it by claiming that such data are irrelevant to understanding and interpreting the plays and poems.

So, what do we know about William Shakespeare, the man responsible for thirty-seven or perhaps more plays, more than 150 sonnets, two lengthy narrative poems, and some shorter poems?

While many families by the name of Shakespeare (or some variant spelling) can be identified in the English Midlands as far back as the twelfth century, it seems likely that the dramatist's grandfather, Richard, moved to Snitterfield, a town not far from Stratford-upon-Avon, sometime before 1529. In Snitterfield, Richard Shakespeare leased farmland from the very wealthy Robert Arden. By 1552, Richard's son John had moved to a large house on Henley Street in Stratford-upon-Avon, the house that stands today as "The Birthplace." In Stratford, John Shakespeare traded as a glover, dealt in wool, and lent money at interest; he also served in a variety of civic posts, including "High Bailiff," the municipality's equivalent of mayor. In 1557, he married Robert Arden's youngest daughter, Mary. Mary and John had four sons – William was the oldest – and four daughters, of whom only Joan outlived her most celebrated sibling. William was baptized (an event entered in the Stratford parish church records) on April 26, 1564, and it has become customary, without any good factual support, to suppose he was born on April 23, which happens to be the feast day of Saint George, patron saint of England, and is also the date on which he died, in 1616. Shakespeare married Anne Hathaway in 1582, when he was eighteen and she was twenty-six; their first child was born five months later. It has been generally assumed that the marriage was enforced and subsequently unhappy, but these are only assumptions; it has been estimated, for instance, that up to one third of Elizabethan brides were pregnant when they married. Anne and William Shakespeare had three children: Susanna, who married a prominent local physician, John Hall; and the twins Hamnet, who died young in 1596, and Judith, who married Thomas Quiney – apparently a rather shady individual. The name Hamnet was unusual but not unique: he and his twin sister were named for their godparents, Shakespeare's neighbors Hamnet and Judith Sadler. Shakespeare's father died in 1601 (the year of *Hamlet*), and Mary Arden Shakespeare died in 1608 (the year of *Coriolanus*). William Shakespeare's last surviving direct descendant was his granddaughter Elizabeth Hall, who died in 1670.

Between the birth of the twins in 1585 and a clear reference to Shakespeare as a practicing London dramatist in Robert Greene's sensationalizing, satiric pamphlet, *Greene's Groatsworth of Wit* (1592), there is no record of where William Shakespeare was or what he was doing. These seven so-called lost years have been imaginatively filled by scholars and other students of Shakespeare: some think he traveled to Italy, or fought in the Low Countries, or studied law or medicine, or worked as an apprentice actor/writer, and so on to even more fanciful possibilities. Whatever the biographical facts for those "lost" years, Greene's nasty remarks in 1592 testify to professional envy and to the fact that Shakespeare already had a successful career in London. Speaking to his fellow playwrights, Greene warns both generally and specifically:

> . . . trust them [actors] not: for there is an upstart crow, beautified with our feathers, that with his tiger's heart wrapped in a player's hide supposes he is as well able to bombast out a blank verse as the best of you; and being an absolute Johannes Factotum, is in his own conceit the only Shake-scene in a country.

The passage mimics a line from *3 Henry VI* (hence the play must have been performed before Greene wrote) and seems to say that "Shake-scene" is both actor and play-wright, a jack-of-all-trades. That same year, Henry Chettle protested Greene's remarks in *Kind-Heart's Dream,* and each of the next two years saw the publication of poems – *Venus and Adonis* and *The Rape of Lucrece,* respectively – publicly ascribed to (and dedicated by) Shakespeare. Early in 1595 he was named one of the senior members of a prominent acting company, the Lord Chamberlain's Men, when they received payment for court performances during the 1594 Christmas season.

Clearly, Shakespeare had achieved both success and reputation in London. In 1596, upon Shakespeare's application, the College of Arms granted his father the now-familiar coat of arms he had taken the first steps to obtain almost twenty years before, and in 1598, John's son – now permitted to call himself "gentleman" – took a 10 percent share in the new Globe playhouse. In 1597, he bought a substantial bourgeois house, called New Place, in Stratford – the garden remains, but Shakespeare's house, several times rebuilt, was torn down in 1759 – and over the next few years Shakespeare spent large sums buying land and making other investments in the town and its environs. Though he worked in London, his family remained in Stratford, and he seems always to have considered Stratford the home he would eventually return to. Something approaching a disinterested appreciation of Shakespeare's popular and professional status appears in Francis Meres's *Palladis Tamia* (1598), a not especially imaginative and perhaps therefore persuasive record of literary reputations. Reviewing contemporary English writers, Meres lists the titles of many of Shakespeare's plays, including one not now known, *Love's Labor's Won,* and praises his "mellifluous & hony-tongued" "sugred Sonnets," which were then circulating in manuscript (they were first collected in 1609). Meres describes Shakespeare as "one of the best" English playwrights of both comedy and tragedy. In *Remains . . . Concerning Britain* (1605),

William Camden – a more authoritative source than the imitative Meres – calls Shakespeare one of the "most pregnant witts of these our times" and joins him with such writers as Chapman, Daniel, Jonson, Marston, and Spenser. During the first decades of the seventeenth century, publishers began to attribute numerous play quartos, including some non-Shakespearean ones, to Shakespeare, either by name or initials, and we may assume that they deemed Shakespeare's name and supposed authorship, true or false, commercially attractive.

For the next ten years or so, various records show Shakespeare's dual career as playwright and man of the theater in London, and as an important local figure in Stratford. In 1608-9 his acting company – designated the "King's Men" soon after King James had succeeded Queen Elizabeth in 1603 – rented, refurbished, and opened a small interior playing space, the Blackfriars theater, in London, and Shakespeare was once again listed as a substantial sharer in the group of proprietors of the playhouse. By May 11, 1612, however, he describes himself as a Stratford resident in a London lawsuit – an indication that he had withdrawn from day-to-day professional activity and returned to the town where he had always had his main financial interests. When Shakespeare bought a substantial residential building in London, the Blackfriars Gatehouse, close to the theater of the same name, on March 10, 1613, he is recorded as William Shakespeare "of Stratford upon Avon in the county of Warwick, gentleman," and he named several London residents as the building's trustees. Still, he continued to participate in theatrical activity: when the new Earl of Rutland needed an allegorical design to bear as a shield, or *impresa,* at the celebration of King James's Accession Day, March 24, 1613, the earl's accountant recorded a payment of 44 shillings to Shakespeare for the device with its motto.

For the last few years of his life, Shakespeare evidently

concentrated his activities in the town of his birth. Most of the final records concern business transactions in Stratford, ending with the notation of his death on April 23, 1616, and burial in Holy Trinity Church, Stratford-upon-Avon.

THE QUESTION OF AUTHORSHIP

The history of ascribing Shakespeare's plays (the poems do not come up so often) to someone else began, as it continues, peculiarly. The earliest published claim that someone else wrote Shakespeare's plays appeared in an 1856 article by Delia Bacon in the American journal *Putnam's Monthly* – although an Englishman, Thomas Wilmot, had shared his doubts in private (even secretive) conversations with friends near the end of the eighteenth century. Bacon's was a sad personal history that ended in madness and poverty, but the year after her article, she published, with great difficulty and the bemused assistance of Nathaniel Hawthorne (then United States Consul in Liverpool, England), her *Philosophy of the Plays of Shakspere Unfolded.* This huge, ornately written, confusing farrago is almost unreadable; sometimes its intents, to say nothing of its arguments, disappear entirely beneath near-raving, ecstatic writing. Tumbled in with much supposed "philosophy" appear the claims that Francis Bacon (from whom Delia Bacon eventually claimed descent), Walter Ralegh, and several other contemporaries of Shakespeare's had written the plays. The book had little impact except as a ridiculed curiosity.

Once proposed, however, the issue gained momentum among people whose conviction was the greater in proportion to their ignorance of sixteenth- and seventeenth-century English literature, history, and society. Another American amateur, Catherine P. Ashmead Windle, made the next influential contribution to the cause when she published *Report to the British Museum* (1882), wherein she promised to open "the Cipher of Francis Bacon," though what she mostly offers, in the words of S. Schoenbaum, is "demented allegorizing." An entire new cottage industry grew from Windle's suggestion that the texts contain hidden, cryptographically discoverable ciphers – "clues" – to their authorship; and today there are not only books devoted to the putative ciphers, but also pamphlets, journals, and newsletters.

Although Baconians have led the pack of those seeking a substitute Shakespeare, in *"Shakespeare" Identified* (1920), J. Thomas Looney became the first published "Oxfordian" when he proposed Edward de Vere, seventeenth earl of Oxford, as the secret author of Shakespeare's plays. Also for Oxford and his "authorship" there are today dedicated societies, articles, journals, and books. Less popular candidates – Queen Elizabeth and Christopher Marlowe among them – have had adherents, but the movement seems to have divided into two main contending factions, Baconian and Oxfordian. (For further details on all the candidates for "Shakespeare," see S. Schoenbaum, *Shakespeare's Lives,* 2nd ed., 1991.)

The Baconians, the Oxfordians, and supporters of other candidates have one trait in common – they are snobs. Every pro-Bacon or pro-Oxford tract sooner or later claims that the historical William Shakespeare of Stratford-upon-Avon could not have written the plays because he could not have had the training, the university education, the experience, and indeed the imagination or background their author supposedly possessed. Only a learned genius like Bacon or an aristocrat like Oxford could have written such fine plays. (As it happens, lucky male children of the middle class had access to better education than most aristocrats in Elizabethan England – and Oxford was not particularly well educated.) Shakespeare received in the Stratford grammar school a formal education that would daunt many college graduates today; and popular rival playwrights such as the very learned Ben Jonson and George Chapman, both of whom also lacked university training, achieved great artistic success, without being taken as Bacon or Oxford.

Besides snobbery, one other quality characterizes the authorship controversy: lack of evidence. A great deal of testimony from Shakespeare's time shows that Shakespeare wrote Shakespeare's plays and that his contemporaries recognized them as distinctive and distinctly superior. (Some of that contemporary evidence is collected in E. K. Chambers, *William Shakespeare: A Study of Facts and Problems,* 2 vols., 1930.) Since that testimony comes from Shakespeare's enemies and theatrical competitors as well as from his co-workers and from the Elizabethan equivalent of literary journalists, it seems unlikely that, if any one of these sources had known he was a fraud, they would have failed to record that fact.

Books About Shakespeare's Theater

Useful scholarly studies of theatrical life in Shakespeare's day include: G. E. Bentley, *The Jacobean and Caroline Stage,* 7 vols. (1941-68), and the same author's *The Professions of Dramatist and Player in Shakespeare's Time, 1590-1642* (1986); E. K. Chambers, *The Elizabethan Stage,* 4 vols. (1923); R. A. Foakes, *Illustrations of the English Stage, 1580-1642* (1985); Andrew Gurr, *The Shakespearean Stage,* 3rd ed. (1992), and the same author's *Play-going in Shakespeare's London,* 2nd ed. (1996); Edwin Nungezer, *A Dictionary of Actors* (1929); Carol Chillington Rutter, ed., *Documents of the Rose Playhouse* (1984).

Books About Shakespeare's Life

The following books provide scholarly, documented accounts of Shakespeare's life: G. E. Bentley, *Shakespeare: A Biographical Handbook* (1961); E. K. Chambers, *William Shakespeare: A Study of Facts and Problems,* 2 vols. (1930); S. Schoenbaum, *William Shakespeare: A Compact*

Documentary Life (1977); and *Shakespeare's Lives,* 2nd ed. (1991), by the same author. Many scholarly editions of Shakespeare's complete works print brief compilations of essential dates and events. References to Shakespeare's works up to 1700 are collected in C. M. Ingleby et al., *The Shakespeare Allusion-Book,* rev. ed., 2 vols. (1932).

The Texts of Shakespeare

As far as we know, only one manuscript conceivably in Shakespeare's own hand may (and even this is much disputed) exist: a few pages of a play called *Sir Thomas More*, which apparently was never performed. What we do have, as later readers, performers, scholars, students, are printed texts. The earliest of these survive in two forms: quartos and folios. Quartos (from the Latin for "four") are small books, printed on sheets of paper that were then folded in fours, to make eight double-sided pages. When these were bound together, the result was a squarish, eminently portable volume that sold for the relatively small sum of sixpence (translating in modern terms to about $5.00). In folios, on the other hand, the sheets are folded only once, in half, producing large, impressive volumes taller than they are wide. This was the format for important works of philosophy, science, theology, and literature (the major precedent for a folio Shakespeare was Ben Jonson's *Works*, 1616). The decision to print the works of a popular playwright in folio is an indication of how far up on the social scale the theatrical profession had come during Shakespeare's lifetime. The Shakespeare folio was an expensive book, selling for between fifteen and eighteen shillings, depending on the binding (in modern terms, from about $150 to $180). Twenty Shakespeare plays of the thirty-seven that survive first appeared in quarto, seventeen of which appeared during Shakespeare's lifetime; the rest of the plays are found only in folio.

The First Folio was published in 1623, seven years after Shakespeare's death, and was authorized by his fellow actors, the co-owners of the King's Men. This publication was certainly a mark of the company's enormous respect for Shakespeare; but it was also a way of turning the old plays, most of which were no longer current in the playhouse, into ready money (the folio includes only Shakespeare's plays, not his sonnets or other nondramatic verse). Whatever the motives behind the publication of the folio, the texts it preserves constitute the basis for almost all later editions of the playwright's works. The texts, however, differ from those of the earlier quartos, sometimes in minor respects but often significantly – most strikingly in the two texts of *King Lear,* but also in important ways in *Hamlet, Othello,* and *Troilus and Cressida.* (The variants are recorded in the textual notes to each play in the new Pelican series.) The differences in these texts represent, in a sense, the essence of theater: the texts of plays were initially not intended for publication. They were scripts, designed for the actors to perform – the principal life of the play at this period was in performance. And it follows that in Shakespeare's theater the playwright typically had no say either in how his play was performed or in the disposition of his text – he was an employee of the company. The authoritative figures in the theatrical enterprise were the shareholders in the company, who were for the most part the major actors. They decided what plays were to be done; they hired the playwright and often gave him an outline of the play they wanted him to write. Often, too, the play was a collaboration: the company would retain a group of writers, and parcel out the scenes among them. The resulting script was then the property of the company, and the actors would revise it as they saw fit during the course of putting it on stage. The resulting text belonged to the company. The playwright had no rights in it once he had been paid. (This system survives largely intact in the movie industry, and most of the playwrights of Shakespeare's time were as anonymous as most screenwriters are today.) The script could also, of course, continue to change as the tastes of audiences and the requirements of the actors changed. Many – perhaps most – plays were revised when they were reintroduced after any substantial absence from the repertory, or when they were performed by a company different from the one that originally commissioned the play.

Shakespeare was an exceptional figure in this world because he was not only a shareholder and actor in his company, but also its leading playwright – he was literally his own boss. He had, moreover, little interest in the publication of his plays, and even those that appeared during his lifetime with the authorization of the company show no signs of any editorial concern on the part of the author. Theater was, for Shakespeare, a fluid and supremely responsive medium – the very opposite of the great classic canonical text that has embodied his works since 1623.

The very fluidity of the original texts, however, has meant that Shakespeare has always had to be edited. Here is an example of how problematic the editorial project inevitably is, a passage from the most famous speech in *Romeo and Juliet,* Juliet's balcony soliloquy beginning "O Romeo, Romeo, wherefore art thou Romeo?" Since the eighteenth century, the standard modern text has read,

> What's Montague? It is nor hand, nor foot,
> Nor arm, nor face, nor any other part
> Belonging to a man. O be some other name!
> What's in a name? That which we call a rose
> By any other name would smell as sweet.
>
> (II.2.40-44)

Editors have three early texts of this play to work from, two quarto texts and the folio. Here is how the First Quarto (1597) reads:

> Whats *Mountague?* It is nor hand nor foote,
> Nor arme, nor face, nor any other part.
> Whats in a name? That which we call a Rose,
> By any other name would smell as sweet:

Here is the Second Quarto (1599):

> Whats *Mountague?* it is nor hand nor foote,
> Nor arme nor face, ô be some other name
> Belonging to a man.
> Whats in a name that which we call a rose,
> By any other word would smell as sweete,

And here is the First Folio (1623):

> What's *Mountague?* it is nor hand nor foote,
> Nor arme, nor face, O be some other name
> Belonging to a man.
> What? in a names that which we call a Rose,
> By any other word would smell as sweete,

There is in fact no early text that reads as our modern text does – and this is the most famous speech in the play. Instead, we have three quite different texts, all of which are clearly some version of the same speech, but none of which seems to us a final or satisfactory version. The transcendently beautiful passage in modern editions is an editorial invention: editors have succeeded in conflating and revising the three versions into something we recognize as great poetry. Is this what Shakespeare "really" wrote? Who can say? What we can say is that Shakespeare always had performance, not a book, in mind.

Books About the Shakespeare Texts

The standard study of the printing history of the First Folio is W. W. Greg, *The Shakespeare First Folio* (1955). J. K. Walton, *The Quarto Copy for the First Folio of Shakespeare* (1971), is a useful survey of the relation of the quartos to the folio. The second edition of Charlton Hinman's *Norton Facsimile* of the First Folio (1996), with a new introduction by Peter Blayney, is indispensable. Stanley Wells and Gary Taylor, *William Shakespeare: A Textual Companion,* keyed to the Oxford text, gives a comprehensive survey of the editorial situation for all the plays and poems.

THE GENERAL EDITORS

Introduction

AT THE CLIMAX OF *Romeo and Juliet,* Romeo dies too soon. Friar Laurence, rushing to prevent Juliet waking alone in the tomb, discovers Romeo's corpse, the "lamentable chance" that "an unkind hour" has caused (V.3.145-46). Juliet does not wake alone: Friar Laurence is there to answer her first question: "where is my lord?" (V.3.148). At the climax of David Garrick's adaptation of *Romeo and Juliet,* first performed at the Theatre Royal, Drury Lane, on November 29, 1748, Juliet wakes up in the tomb before Friar Laurence arrives but also, much more significantly, before Romeo has died. Romeo, forgetting for the moment that he has already taken the poison and is dying, is in raptures: "She speaks, she lives! And we shall still be blessed!" For a brief moment, the lovers' passion seems able to conquer the threat of impending death. But the poison has taken hold and Romeo, explaining to Juliet what has happened, cannot resist its power and dies.

Garrick was not the first to make this change. In 1679 Thomas Otway had given the lovers a final pathetic dialogue in his adaptation, *The History and Fall of Caius Marius,* which transposed the action to ancient Rome. It was there too in Theophilus Cibber's version performed in 1744. As Garrick recognized, this final and desperate love duet had been present in the story of Romeo and Juliet in some of the versions that preceded Shakespeare's – in Luigi da Porto's narrative, first published in 1530, and in Matteo Bandello's novella of 1554. When Pierre Boiastuau adapted Bandello and translated it from Italian into French in 1559, he altered the events at this point and his Romeo dies before Juliet wakes up. It was Boiastuau's account that was translated into English in

1567 by William Painter in his *Palace of Pleasure* and that formed the basis for the long narrative poem by Arthur Brooke, *The Tragical History of Romeus and Juliet,* published in 1562, Shakespeare's primary source for the play.

Garrick argued, in the preface to the 1753 edition of his adaptation, that Shakespeare had not explored the opportunity for such a moving scene, "not perhaps from judgement, but from reading the story in the French or English translation, both which have injudiciously left out this addition to the catastrophe." The need for the lovers to have some kind of living contact in the tomb and for the action's "catastrophe" to be played out against that horrifyingly short and illusory vision of escaping the workings of fate did not end with Garrick. But giving the lovers a shared moment in the tomb scene can take on other emphases. In Baz Luhrmann's 1996 film version, *William Shakespeare's Romeo + Juliet,* Juliet wakes just a few seconds too late and sees Romeo take the poison though she cannot prevent it. Appalled, the lovers have to share the recognition that nothing can be done, that Romeo will die and that Juliet must watch him die.

Garrick found in the problem of the sources an explanation for Shakespeare's failure to write a final scene for the two lovers, a scene that for Garrick would have been of "more nature, terror and distress." But it is worth wondering whether Shakespeare would have wanted such a scene anyway. After all, if Garrick was able to see what such a scene would do, so too could Shakespeare have done and he certainly did not slavishly follow the material in any source he ever used. The scene as Shakespeare wrote it is a desolate series of gaps and mistakes. As such it brings to an apt conclusion the gaps and errors that have impelled it into being, one more part of the play's explorations of the tragedy of incompletion.

Throughout *Romeo and Juliet* there is a tension between the possibilities of patterning and order and the recognition of the temporary and evanescent nature of such possibilities. The order is epitomized in the play's teasing games with the formalities of poetic shape embodied in a sonnet. After the publication of Sir Philip Sidney's sonnet cycle *Astrophil and Stella* in 1591, English poets responded with a craze for sonneteering. In the years before Shakespeare wrote *Romeo and Juliet,* probably in 1595, sonnet sequences were published by Daniel, Drayton, Lodge, Spenser, and many more. The form of a sonnet, whatever its particular choice of rhyme scheme, encloses the explosive desire of which the poem tries to speak. As the poet describes the limitless extent of his love, the claim of infinite emotion is held within the rigidity of the formal structure.

Romeo and Juliet opens with a prologue in sonnet form. Its narrative is a careful definition of one way of understanding the drama that it prefigures, seeing the lovers as fated, "star-crossed," "death-marked." In the literary form that most explicitly seeks to evoke love without death, love and death entwine only through Elizabethan sonnets' contemplation of that standard pun on death and orgasm. When the chorus reappears to offer another sonnet, love and death are redefined:

> Now old desire doth in his deathbed lie,
>> And young affection gapes to be his heir
>>> (II.Cho.1-2)

This time the death is not the lovers' death but the death of love, Romeo's love for Rosaline turned into an image of an old man wheezing his last while Romeo's love for Juliet stands expectantly waiting to collect his inheritance. It is a harsher version of Benvolio's earlier advice to Romeo:

> Take thou some new infection to thy eye,
> And the rank poison of the old will die.
>> (I.2.49-50)

Benvolio's lines, a quatrain and the above couplet, suggest a sonnet's ending as he recommends that the cure for love lies in a new object for love, a form of inconstant affection that seems the antithesis of the dedicated lover's obsession with the perfect object of that love, the conventional subject matter for sonnets. But Benvolio's odd fragment of a sonnet is a less bizarre transmutation of the form than the two choruses. Neither chorus is exactly the kind of sonnet one might usually expect of the form in the 1590s; death is too immediate, a threatening presence bound up with the love. In any case, the control of an action that might seem possible through the repeated appearances of a chorus proves to be merely illusory. After the opening of the second act, the chorus will never reappear.

But before the second chorus, Romeo and Juliet have met and spoken. Their first exchange is constructed as a sonnet (I.5.94–107), a shape defined by Romeo's opening quatrain and by his making a final couplet in rhyming with Juliet's line. The creation of the sonnet is a shared activity, perhaps a conscious one (in that they may be aware that they are participating in this act of poetic creativity); it is the lovers' naturally artificial response to the passion that they feel. But it is also a structure that enmeshes them in the enjoyment of the overextension of the imagery of saints and pilgrims. The sonnet is extravagant, controlledly exuberant. Their enjoyment of its pleasurable forms leads them to begin to construct a second sonnet at once. But this time only one quatrain is in place before the nurse interrupts with the summons of Juliet's mother.

The lovers' second sonnet is incomplete. The sequence of sonnet choruses peters out after two. Instead, the overall shaping of the play is suggested by other repetitions: for instance, the bustling preparations in the Capulet household for the feast in I.5 and again for the wedding in IV.4 or, more weightily, the appearances of the prince on three pivotal occasions: after the opening brawl, after the deaths of Tybalt and Mercutio, and in the tomb at the end, in each case following one of the play's three sequences of swordplay. The prince's interventions are an expression of authority but they are strikingly ineffective. Like so much else in *Romeo and Juliet,* authority appears too late; its responses can only be untimely. There may be a fair logic to his actions (for instance, in his refusal to execute Romeo for the murder of Tybalt) but, as he himself worries, he may be at fault for "winking at your discords" (V.3.294). The last six lines of the play, the prince's quatrain and couplet, replicate the end of a sonnet but these lines speak only of "sad things" and "woe," not of love, repeating the poetic form that Paris has used for his lament at Juliet's tomb close to the start of the last scene (V.3.12-17) so that the two sestets frame the final action. They are the play's last fragments of sonnet and in their fragmentary state embody the play's truncated loves. No separated figure, the prince is firmly and painfully implicated in the kinship structures of Verona. Mercutio and Paris are his kinsmen; it is his view – though it may not be ours – that the direct consequence of his failure to exert sufficiently effective authority is that he has "lost a brace of kinsmen" (V.3.295).

The lovers will be memorialized in the gold statues that the two fathers will pay for, an emblem of the parents' feuding turned into competitive symbols for their grieving. Even a public expression of grief now becomes a place to represent wealth. But the feud will have the possibility of a formal end in the handshake that precedes the offer of the statues, and the handshake itself is an expression of a new kind of kinship:

> O brother Montague, give me thy hand.
> This is my daughter's jointure, for no more
> Can I demand.
>
> (V.3.296-98)

Montague and Capulet can now be brothers, not a direct expression of a blood kinship structure but a definition of an emotional bond between them. Yet the brotherhood still involves the transfer of a dowry for the marriage, a dowry that has no monetary value, only a bonding between the two men.

Romeo and Juliet is a tragedy that depends crucially on kinship, and kinship is here an act of naming. The play's most famous line, "O Romeo, Romeo! wherefore art thou Romeo?" (II.2.33), begins Juliet's debate on the possibility of separating Romeo from his name. Yet the problem is not, of course, that he is called Romeo but that he is a Montague. It is not his personal name but his father's name, the name that defines which of the households he belongs to, that causes the problem. In the end, as a corpse in the Capulet monument, he has denied his name, as Juliet asked him to do.

The play is full of characters whose names are solely a definition of allegiance. The two heads of the households, Montague and Capulet, have no names other than their family identities. In the early editions, the character usually known as Lady Capulet is never called that in the play or in the speech prefixes for her lines. Instead the speech prefixes keep changing so that she is, at different times, wife, mother, lady, and old lady. My choice for this edition, Capulet's wife, is an attempt to give consistency where perhaps inconsistency, a shifting place in the structures of relationship, might be a more accurate reflection of Shakespeare's changing ideas about the character. She is known only through her connections with others, without a personal name at all. Even the prince's personal name, Escalus, exists solely in the stage direction for his first entry; the name is never spoken onstage, never heard by the audience.

Every character in Verona, except for the friars, is explicitly aligned with social groupings created by this network of kinship and allegiance. Even the long list of those whom Peter has to invite to Capulet's "old-accustomed feast" (I.2.64-72) has those who "be not of the house of Montagues" (81-82). Perhaps the servingman who cannot identify Juliet for Romeo when he first sees her at the party ("I know not, sir," I.5.44) has just been hired in for the evening. But in the world of the feud, where even to be in a public space is to be threatened (as the nurse is taunted by Mercutio in II.4), the alignments are crucial for the young men. Mercutio may be the prince's relative but he places himself with Romeo, almost as if he were a Montague. It is Mercutio whose desire to fight in III.1 exacerbates Tybalt's readiness to duel. For the feud is sustained by the young men, not by the heads of the households. Montagues may not be invited to Capulet's feast but Tybalt's fury at Romeo's appearance there is harshly held in check by Capulet, who sees nothing offensive in the presence of "a virtuous and well-governed youth" (I.5.69). Whatever may have been the originating cause of the feud, it is continued by the earnest need of the young men to prove their masculinity through their swords. By the end of the play, it is the young men among whom the death toll is highest: Romeo, Paris, Tybalt, and Mercutio. Their deaths are matched in the older generation only by the mysterious death of Montague's wife.

Only Benvolio escapes the general slaughter and he simply vanishes from the play after he has explained to the prince how Mercutio and Tybalt died. In the "bad" quarto of 1597, Montague has an extra line at the end, following his announcement "my wife is dead tonight," to explain what has happened to Benvolio: "and young Benvolio is deceased too." But Shakespeare did not choose to tie up this loose end. Instead, the man whose name so fully describes his function, the one who wishes well, has no further place in the action as the potential for a comic resolution is eradicated by the deaths of Mercutio and Tybalt.

In the play's complex system of balances, Mercutio is in some ways the counterpart of the nurse. As she is Juliet's confidante, so he is Romeo's intimate friend. Both have a propensity for sexual punning, consciously in Mercutio's case, perhaps largely unconsciously in the nurse's. Their bawdy humor is set against the high-flown romantic love, the rhapsodic intensity of desire between Romeo and Juliet. While Romeo is overwhelmed by the new quality of love that his feelings toward Juliet create, a love that can proceed only through marriage, Mercutio turns love into the much simpler desire for sex, mocking the rhetoric of love by encouraging the propensity of language to refer punningly to genital sex.

Such obscenity and such wordplay were too much for David Garrick's audience, and Garrick felt himself obliged "to clear the original as much as possible from the jingle and quibble," but he could not effectively eradicate quibbles from a play in which wordplay is indissolubly part of the fabric of the language, in which tropes and puns are part of each character's attempt to impose order on the disorder of life in Verona. Mercutio, however, revels in that spiraling lack of control. He can be as rhapsodic as the lovers but his imaginative power creates new worlds, fantasies like Queen Mab that deny the foreboding dreams of Romeo. As the nurse's advice to Juliet to marry Paris isolates Juliet, leaving her with no friend to turn to when she most needs help, so Romeo loses Mercutio. But Mercutio has already lost Romeo through Romeo's falling in love with Juliet.

Many characters spend time in the play looking for Romeo. Mercutio is not the only one to wonder "Where the devil should this Romeo be?" (II.4.1). Even before his first appearance his parents are wondering where he is. Romeo never speaks with his parents; he no sooner makes his first entrance than Benvolio advises them to leave (I.1.155–56). As a young man, Romeo can go where he pleases in Verona. Juliet, by contrast, as a young unmarried woman, is firmly kept indoors. She even needs permission to go to Friar Laurence for confession, as the nurse asks her "Have you got leave to go to shrift today?" (II.5.66). The friar's cell is the only place at which Montague and Capulet can meet without aggression.

But Friar Laurence is a troubling figure in the play. Twice the play moves from sword fight to the arrival of the prince to a narrative of explanation by Benvolio. At the third example of the pattern the narrative is offered by the friar (V.3.229-69). Where Benvolio had little personal stake in his accounts, the friar's lengthy recapitulation of the events of the drama is driven by his sense of his guilt. He may propose to be "brief" but the tale requires such a long retelling. Often abbreviated or cut completely in modern productions, the friar's apologia is another part of the play's exploration of responsibility. When Romeo's intervention had led to Tybalt's stabbing Mercutio under Romeo's arm, Romeo can honestly respond "I thought all for the best" (III.1.103) and his desolate cry could also stand for the actions of many other characters – for instance, the nurse's advising Juliet to marry Paris ("I think it best you married with the county," III.5.219). But it is the friar who most often advises a particular course of action in order to engineer a particular consequence: the marriage of Romeo and Juliet will, he hopes, "so happy prove / To turn your households' rancor to pure love" (II.3.91-92).

For Arthur Brooke, Shakespeare's prime source, the purpose of his poem could be expressed in fiercely moralistic tones:

> And to this end (good reader) is this tragical matter written to describe unto thee a couple of unfortunate lovers, thralling themselves to unhonest desire, neglecting the authority and advice of parents and friends, conferring their principal counsels with drunken gossips and superstitious friars (the naturally fit instruments of unchastity), attempting all adventures of peril for th'attaining of their wished lust,

using auricular confession (the key of whoredom and treason) for the furtherance of their purpose, abusing the honourable name of lawful marriage (the cloak the shame of stolen contracts), finally, by all means of unhonest life, hasting to most unhappy death.

To be fair, Brooke's poem is often in intriguing tension with his moral assertions but, as Shakespeare rethought and reworked Brooke's "tragical history" into his "most excellent and lamentable tragedy" (as the 1599 quarto's title page describes it), there is no space left for anti-Catholic dismissal of friars and confessions (or for seeing the lovers' desire as "unhonest," the nurse as a "drunken gossip," or the wedding as "abusing the honourable name of lawful marriage"). Friar Laurence's integrity is unquestioned but his rational approach to each problem posed him can only show how conclusively the operation of chance works against human plans. The prince's single line of response to the friar's outpouring of self-incriminatory guilt reassures us – though not perhaps Friar Laurence – of his good intentions as well as of the inadequacies of such good intentions in the dangerous world of human experience: "We still have known thee for a holy man" (V.3.270).

Friar Laurence's narrative looks back over the events of the play but characters also often look forward. The play is full of premonitory warning. Romeo's anxiety before going to the Capulet feast is only too accurate: the act of going does indeed lead to a consequence that ends with his "untimely death" (I.4.111). But all such actions are bound up with the concept of the opportune moment. Benvolio worries, "we shall come too late"; Romeo worries that they will be "too early" (105-6). The accident of Friar Laurence's letter never reaching Romeo in Mantua leads Romeo to return to Verona too early and Friar Laurence to arrive at the tomb too late. Over and over again the drama moves from the possibility of a happy ending to its appalling catastrophe by the tiniest of temporal margins. Friar Laurence's clichéd advice to Romeo, "Wisely and slow. They stumble that run fast" (II.3.94), proves true but in the breathless haste of the drama there is no time to act slowly. Juliet senses in the balcony scene that their contract is "too rash, too unadvised, too sudden" (II.2.118) but there is no other choice available to them. Even Friar Laurence's attempts to manipulate time cannot work: the potion he gives Juliet proves only to accelerate the transformation of the illusion of death into its reality.

One of Shakespeare's transformations of Brooke's plot is a radical compression of its time scheme. Where in Brooke the lovers meet for the second time "a week or two" after their first meeting, in Shakespeare it is the same night; where Brooke allowed them, after their marriage, to meet each night "for a month or twain," in Shakespeare they have a single night together. Brooke's spacious slow-paced narrative becomes a drama that cannot halt its headlong career. It is only too characteristic of the dramatic pace that Juliet should want the day to end quickly: "Gallop apace, you fiery-footed steeds, / Towards Phoebus' lodging!" (III.2.1-2). The characters, especially Juliet's father, are pressingly aware of the days of the week. The events of the play take place in mid-July, "A fortnight and odd days" before "Lammastide," August 1 (I.3.15), starting on a Sunday and ending early on Thursday morning. The action occurs in the middle of the month most appropriate for someone called Juliet, who was born on Lammas Eve, July 31, in the last hours of the month she is named after, another part of the play's squeezing of time's boundaries to their limits. The audience is continually being reminded of the time of day, the diurnal rhythm that provides its own structures for the action: Romeo and Juliet's three scenes of love – at the feast, at the balcony (when Romeo wants to climb up), and at their parting (when Romeo must climb down) – which together chart a movement from evening through night to dawn, the parallel intensified by the way that the nurse interrupts them on each occasion, forcing the lovers to part.

Throughout, the lovers have to fight to find their brief moments of time and space, and their delight in those moments is always circumscribed by their awareness of the necessary brevity, their consciousness that they cannot sustain the moment of contact. But their contact has a quality of the absolute about it that has turned Romeo and Juliet into Western culture's epitome of love – heterosexual, adolescent, secret, foredoomed.

Romeo may go to the Capulet feast simply to see Rosaline (and many modern productions have turned Shakespeare's unseen figure into a visible presence there) but, once Juliet is seen, Rosaline is forgotten. The audience at David Garrick's 1748 version of the play "thought that the sudden change of Romeo's love from Rosaline to Juliet was a blemish in his character," as Garrick wrote in his preface to the 1750 version of the text, which eliminated all reference to Rosaline, even though, as Garrick knew, "to be young and inconstant was extremely natural." The name "Romeo" has come to be used for what the Oxford English Dictionary sternly describes as "a seducer, a habitual pursuer of women," as if Romeo is defined by the change of the object of desire. The love for Rosaline seems the stuff of comedy but, like so much else in *Romeo and Juliet,* the materials change and comedy turns inexorably into tragedy. Where Shakespeare's previous (and indeed subsequent) tragedies never entertain the possibility of belonging to any other genre, *Romeo and Juliet* teases the audience with the possibility of comedy. But the chances for comedy are progressively eradicated by the changes in the action. After Mercutio's death, in particular, comedy turns into bitter situational irony, like the painfully prolonged cross-purposes conversation between the nurse and Juliet over whether it is Tybalt or Romeo who has been killed (III.2.32-70), or the way the bed in which Romeo and Juliet consummate their marriage becomes the bed in which Juliet fakes death and then, in the metamorphosis of staging, the bier in the tomb on which she will die indeed. The change of love object from Rosaline to Juliet seems, in retrospect, the first step toward tragedy; it is a change of desire that we want to find irreversible and cataclysmic.

Shakespeare's Juliet may be younger than his sources' – not yet fourteen compared with eighteen in Painter and sixteen in Brooke – but she has an intelligence and maturity Brooke and Painter did not allow for. Forced to reject the nurse when she advises marriage to Paris, Juliet turns to Friar Laurence as a last resort. Her statement "If all else fail, myself have power to die" (III.5.244) has a calm assurance that convinces us it is no empty threat. Where Brooke's Juliet faints at the news of Tybalt's death, Shakespeare's explores her emotions with profound acuity. Her love for Romeo and desire to love him had been "boundless as the sea" (II.2.133); now she finds "no end, no limit, measure, bound" (III.2.125) in the news of his banishment. Montague and Capulet were "bound" to keep the peace (I.2.1) but Juliet's extremes of experience are boundless. Mercutio wanted Romeo to "Borrow Cupid's wings / And soar with them above a common bound" (I.4.17-18) but it is Juliet who seems most able to do so. Where the community seeks to bind the actions of the warring households or encodes female behavior within "the bounds of modesty" (IV.2.27), the individual might be forced to feel something beyond bounds, as marriage between Capulet daughter and Montague son is itself out of bounds.

Romeo and Juliet is not the play that its popular image has created. It is not a great romantic tragedy of love duets of the kind Garrick chose to add. Yet the consolation Friar Laurence offers Juliet's parents, fiancé, and nurse after their operatic scene of lamentation over her supposed

corpse – consolation that he knows not really to be necessary – may strike audiences as wry, perhaps painfully
ironic in its figuring of the play's true end.

> She's not well married that lives married long,
> But she's best married that dies married young.
> (IV.5.77-78)

In a play in which so much happens too soon or too late,
the intensity with which Romeo and Juliet snatch time
together may seem scant consolation but the only consolation possible.

PETER HOLLAND
The Shakespeare Institute,
The University of Birmingham

Note on the Text

THE ONLY DEPARTURES from the copy text (Second Quarto, 1599) are listed below, except for relineations, corrections of obvious typographical errors, added stage directions (in brackets), and the treatment of canceled passages (explained in the notes). Variants in speech prefixes within a scene have been regularized without comment. All the listed readings have been adopted from the First Quarto, 1597, except those marked Q3 (Third Quarto, 1609), Q4 (Fourth Quarto, 1623), F1 (First Folio, 1623), F2 (Second Folio, 1632), F3 (Third Folio, 1664), F4 (Fourth Folio, 1683), and Eds (emendation, usually made quite early in the history of Shakespearean textual study and still generally accepted by modern editors). The adopted reading in italics is followed by the reading of the copy text in roman.

I.1   26 *in sense* sense   30 *comes two* comes   146 *his* is   152 *sun* (Eds) same   176 *create* created   178 *well-seeming* (Q4) well-seeing   201 *Bid a sick* A sick;   *make* makes   202 *Ah* A   210 *unharmed* uncharmed   217 *makes* (Q4) make
I.2   66 Vitruvio (F3) Vtruuio   70 *and Livia* Livia   75–76 *Whither? /* PETER *To supper* to (Eds) Whether to supper? / *Ser.* To
I.3   66, 67 *honor* hour   99 *make it fly* make fly
I.4   23 MERCUTIO (Q4) Horatio.   39 *done* dum   42 *Of this sir-reverence* Or save you reverence   45 *like lamps* lights lights   47 *five* fine   66 *maid* man   72 *O'er courtiers'* On courtiers   76 *breaths* breath   81 *dreams he* he dreams   113 *sail* suit
I.5   17 *a bout* (Eds) about   18 *Ah ha* Ah   96 *ready* did ready
II.Cho.   4 *matched* (Q3) match
II.1   10 *pronounce* prouaunt;   *dove* day   12 *heir* her   13 *trim* true   38 *open-arse and* (Eds) open, or
II.2   31 *pacing* puffing   41–42 *nor any . . . name* (Eds) ô be some other name / Belonging to a man (Q2); nor any other part. (Q1)   45 *were* wene   83 *washed* washeth   99 *havior* behavior   101 *more cunning* coying   110 *circled* circle   163 *mine* (Q2 omits)   164 *my Romeo's*

name. Romeo! my Romeo.   **179** *her* his   **188** (Q2 adds 4 lines nearly identical to II.3.1–4; see note in text)   **189** *sire's close* (Eds) friar's close

II.3   2 *Check'ring* (Q2 in version at end of II.2) Checking   **4** *fiery* burning   **22** *sometime's* sometime   **26** *slays* stays   **74** *ring yet* yet ringing

II.4   18 s.p. BENVOLIO Romeo   **19** *I can tell you* (Q2 omits)   **29** *phantasims* (Eds) phantacies   **110** *for* (Q2 omits)   **193** *I warrant* (F2) Warrant   **204** *dog's* (Q3) dog.

II.5   11 *three* (Q3) there

III.1   2 *Capels are* Capels   **90** *both your* (Eds) both   **107** *soundly too. Your* (Eds) soundly, to your   **121** *Alive* He gan   **123** *eyed* end   **165** *agile* aged   **183 s.p.** MONTAGUE (Q4) Capu.   **187** *hate's* hearts   **191** *I* It

III.2   9 *By* (Q4) And by   **51** *determine of* (F1) determine   **76** *Dove-feathered* (Eds) Ravenous dove-feathered   **79** *damnèd* (Q4) dimme

III.3   15 *Hence* Here   **52** *Thou* Then   **61** *madmen* madman   **110** *denote* devote   **117** *lives* (F4) lies   **138** *happy too* happy   **144** *pout'st upon* (Q4) puts up   **168** *disguised* (Q3) disguise

III.4   23 *We'll* well   **34** *very very* very

III.5   13 *exhales* exhale   **43** *my* ay   **83** *pardon him* (Q4) pardon   **140** *gives* (Q3) give   **173 s.p.** CAPULET Father (as part of Nurse's speech)   **182** *lined* (Eds) liand; trained (Q1)

IV.1   45 *cure* care   **72** *slay* stay   **83** *chapless* chapels   **85** *his shroud* (Q4) his   **98** *breath* breast   **100** *wanny* (Eds) many   **110** *In* (Q3) Is   **116** *waking* (Q3) walking

IV.4   21 *faith* (Q4) father

IV.5   41 *long* love   **65** *cure* (Eds) care   **81** *In all* And in   **82** *fond* (F2) some   **104** *full of woe* (Q4) full   **120 s.p.** PETER (before "I" in Q2)   **123** *grief* griefs   **130, 133** *Pretty* Prates

V.1   15 *fares my* doth my Lady   **24** *defy* deny   **76** *pay* pray

V.3   3 *yew tree* young trees   **68** *conjurations* commiration   **137** *yew* (Eds) young   **190** *shrieked* (Eds) shrike   **209** *more early* now earling   **232** *that* thats   **299** *raise* (Q4) raie

Romeo and Juliet

[NAMES OF THE ACTORS

CHORUS
ROMEO
MONTAGUE, *his father*
MONTAGUE'S WIFE
BENVOLIO, *Montague's nephew*
ABRAM, *Montague's servingman*
BALTHASAR, *Romeo's servingman*
JULIET
CAPULET, *her father*
CAPULET'S WIFE
TYBALT, *her nephew*
TYBALT'S PAGE
PETRUCCIO
CAPULET'S COUSIN
JULIET'S NURSE
PETER ⎫
SAMPSON ⎪
GREGORY ⎬ *servingmen of the Capulets*
ANTHONY ⎪
POTPAN ⎭
OTHER SERVINGMEN
MUSICIANS
ESCALUS, *Prince of Verona*
MERCUTIO ⎫ *his kinsmen*
COUNTY PARIS ⎭
PARIS'S PAGE
FRIAR LAURENCE
FRIAR JOHN
AN APOTHECARY
CHIEF WATCHMAN
OTHER CITIZENS OF THE WATCH
MASKERS, GUESTS, GENTLEWOMEN, SUPPORTERS
  OF THE MONTAGUE AND CAPULET HOUSES

SCENE: *Verona, Mantua*]
*

Romeo and Juliet

∾ **The Prologue**

[Enter] Chorus.

CHORUS

Two households, both alike in dignity,   1
   In fair Verona, where we lay our scene,
From ancient grudge break to new mutiny,   3
   Where civil blood makes civil hands unclean.   4
From forth the fatal loins of these two foes
   A pair of star-crossed lovers take their life;   6
Whose misadventured piteous overthrows   7
   Doth with their death bury their parents' strife.
The fearful passage of their death-marked love,   9
   And the continuance of their parents' rage,   10
Which, but their children's end, naught could remove,
   Is now the two hours' traffic of our stage;   12
The which if you with patient ears attend,
What here shall miss, our toil shall strive to mend.   14

                                           [Exit.]

*

Pro. (The prologue is in the form of a sonnet.) 1 *dignity* rank 3 *mutiny* outbursts of violence 4 *civil . . . civil* citizens' . . . fellow citizens' 6 *star-crossed* thwarted by adverse stars 7 *misadventured* unlucky 9 *death-marked* foredoomed to death 12 *two . . . stage* our stage business for the next two hours 14 *miss* go wrong; *mend* amend (next time)

∾ **I.1** *Enter Sampson and Gregory, with swords and bucklers, of the house of Capulet.*

1 SAMPSON   Gregory, on my word, we'll not carry coals.

2 GREGORY   No, for then we should be colliers.

3 SAMPSON   I mean, an we be in choler, we'll draw.

4 GREGORY   Ay, while you live, draw your neck out of collar.

SAMPSON   I strike quickly, being moved.

GREGORY   But thou art not quickly moved to strike.

SAMPSON   A dog of the house of Montague moves me.

GREGORY   To move is to stir, and to be valiant is to stand. Therefore, if thou art moved, thou runn'st away.

10 SAMPSON   A dog of that house shall move me to stand. I

11 will take the wall of any man or maid of Montague's.

12 GREGORY   That shows thee a weak slave; for the weakest goes to the wall.

SAMPSON   'Tis true; and therefore women, being the

15 weaker vessels, are ever thrust to the wall. Therefore I will push Montague's men from the wall and thrust his maids to the wall.

GREGORY   The quarrel is between our masters, and us their men.

20 SAMPSON   'Tis all one. I will show myself a tyrant. When I have fought with the men, I will be civil with the maids – I will cut off their heads.

GREGORY   The heads of the maids?

SAMPSON   Ay, the heads of the maids, or their maiden-

25 heads. Take it in what sense thou wilt.

GREGORY   They must take it in sense that feel it.

I.1 A public place in Verona **s.d.** *bucklers* small shields   **1** *carry coals* i.e., suffer insults   **2** *colliers* coal dealers   **3** *an* if; *choler* anger; *draw* draw our swords   **4** *collar* hangman's noose   **11** *take the wall* pass on the inner and cleaner part of the sidewalk (not in the gutter)   **12–13** *the weakest . . . wall* i.e., is pushed from his place (proverbial)   **15** *weaker vessels* (cf. I Peter 3:7); *thrust . . . wall* (suggesting a sexual assault)   **25–26** *sense . . . sense* meaning . . . physical sensation

SAMPSON   Me they shall feel while I am able to stand; 27
and 'tis known I am a pretty piece of flesh. 28

GREGORY   'Tis well thou art not fish; if thou hadst, thou
hadst been Poor John. Draw thy tool! Here comes two 30
of the house of Montagues.

Enter two other Servingmen [Abram and Balthasar].

SAMPSON   My naked weapon is out. Quarrel! I will back
thee.

GREGORY   How? turn thy back and run?

SAMPSON   Fear me not.

GREGORY   No, marry. I fear thee! 36

SAMPSON   Let us take the law of our sides; let them begin. 37

GREGORY   I will frown as I pass by, and let them take it as
they list.

SAMPSON   Nay, as they dare. I will bite my thumb at 40
them, which is disgrace to them if they bear it.

ABRAM   Do you bite your thumb at us, sir?

SAMPSON   I do bite my thumb, sir.

ABRAM   Do you bite your thumb at us, sir?

SAMPSON   *[Aside to Gregory]* Is the law of our side if I
say ay?

GREGORY   *[Aside to Sampson]* No.

SAMPSON   No, sir, I do not bite my thumb at you, sir;
but I bite my thumb, sir.

GREGORY   Do you quarrel, sir? 50

ABRAM   Quarrel, sir? No, sir.

SAMPSON   But if you do, sir, I am for you. I serve as good
a man as you.

ABRAM   No better.

---

27 *stand* (punning on "have an erection")   28–29 *flesh . . . fish* (alluding to
the proverb "Neither fish nor flesh"; "flesh" also suggests "penis")   30 *Poor
John* dried hake, the cheapest fish; *tool* sword (punning on "penis," which
Sampson continues in "naked weapon," l. 32)   36 *marry* indeed (originally
an oath, on the name of the Virgin Mary); *I fear thee* to suppose me afraid of
you is ridiculous   37 *take . . . of* have the law on   40 *bite my thumb* (an
insulting gesture)

SAMPSON   Well, sir.
> *Enter Benvolio.*

GREGORY   *[Aside to Sampson]* Say "better." Here comes
one of my master's kinsmen.

SAMPSON   Yes, better, sir.

ABRAM   You lie.

60 SAMPSON   Draw, if you be men. Gregory, remember thy
61 washing blow.
> *They fight.*

BENVOLIO   Part, fools!
Put up your swords. You know not what you do.
> *Enter Tybalt.*

TYBALT
64 What, art thou drawn among these heartless hinds?
Turn thee, Benvolio! look upon thy death.

BENVOLIO
I do but keep the peace. Put up thy sword,
Or manage it to part these men with me.

TYBALT
What, drawn, and talk of peace? I hate the word
As I hate hell, all Montagues, and thee.
70 Have at thee, coward!
> *[They fight.]*
> *Enter [as Officers of the Watch] three or four Citizens*
> *with clubs or partisans.*

71 CITIZENS   Clubs, bills, and partisans! Strike! beat them
down! Down with the Capulets! Down with the
Montagues!
> *Enter old Capulet in his gown, and his Wife.*

CAPULET
What noise is this? Give me my long sword, ho!

CAPULET'S WIFE
A crutch, a crutch! Why call you for a sword?

---

61 *washing* swashing, smashing **64** *heartless hinds* cowardly servants **71**
bills, partisans long-shafted weapons with combined spearhead and cutting
blade **73 s.d.** *gown* dressing gown, robe

CAPULET
   My sword, I say! Old Montague is come
   And flourishes his blade in spite of me.   77
     Enter old Montague and his Wife.
MONTAGUE
   Thou villain Capulet! – Hold me not, let me go.
MONTAGUE'S WIFE
   Thou shalt not stir one foot to seek a foe.
     Enter Prince Escalus, with his train.
PRINCE
   Rebellious subjects, enemies to peace,   80
   Profaners of this neighbor-stainèd steel –
   Will they not hear? What, ho! you men, you beasts,
   That quench the fire of your pernicious rage
   With purple fountains issuing from your veins!
   On pain of torture, from those bloody hands
   Throw your mistempered weapons to the ground   86
   And hear the sentence of your movèd prince.   87
   Three civil brawls, bred of an airy word   88
   By thee, old Capulet, and Montague,
   Have thrice disturbed the quiet of our streets   90
   And made Verona's ancient citizens
   Cast by their grave beseeming ornaments   92
   To wield old partisans, in hands as old,
   Cankered with peace, to part your cankered hate.   94
   If ever you disturb our streets again,
   Your lives shall pay the forfeit of the peace.
   For this time all the rest depart away.
   You, Capulet, shall go along with me;
   And, Montague, come you this afternoon,
   To know our farther pleasure in this case,   *100*

---

77 *in spite of* in defiance of   86 *mistempered* (1) angry, (2) tempered for use
for a bad purpose   87 *movèd* angry   88 *airy* made with breath; trivial   92
grave beseeming ornaments staffs and costumes appropriate for the aged   94
Cankered . . . cankered rusted . . . malignant

101   To old Freetown, our common judgment place.
      Once more, on pain of death, all men depart.
          Exeunt [all but Montague, his Wife, and Benvolio].

MONTAGUE

103   Who set this ancient quarrel new abroach?
      Speak, nephew, were you by when it began?

BENVOLIO

      Here were the servants of your adversary
      And yours, close fighting ere I did approach.
      I drew to part them. In the instant came
      The fiery Tybalt, with his sword prepared,
      Which, as he breathed defiance to my ears,

110   He swung about his head and cut the winds,

111   Who, nothing hurt withal, hissed him in scorn.
      While we were interchanging thrusts and blows,
      Came more and more, and fought on part and part,
      Till the prince came, who parted either part.

MONTAGUE'S WIFE

      O, where is Romeo? Saw you him today?
      Right glad I am he was not at this fray.

BENVOLIO

      Madam, an hour before the worshiped sun
      Peered forth the golden window of the east,
      A troubled mind drive me to walk abroad;

120   Where, underneath the grove of sycamore
      That westward rooteth from this city side,
      So early walking did I see your son.

123   Towards him I made, but he was ware of me

124   And stole into the covert of the wood.

125   I, measuring his affections by my own,

---

101 *Freetown* (Arthur Brooke's translation, in his poem *Romeus and Juliet* [1562], of *Villafranca* in Bandello's "Romeo e Giulietta," where it is the name of Capulet's house) **103** *set . . . abroach* reopened this quarrel of long standing **111** *Who* which; *nothing* not at all; *withal* therewith **123** *ware* aware, wary **124** *covert* cover **125** *affections* inclinations, feelings

Which then most sought where most might not be   126
  found,
Being one too many by my weary self,
Pursued my humor, not pursuing his,   128
And gladly shunned who gladly fled from me.

MONTAGUE
Many a morning hath he there been seen,   *130*
With tears augmenting the fresh morning's dew,
Adding to clouds more clouds with his deep sighs;
But all so soon as the all-cheering sun
Should in the farthest east begin to draw
The shady curtains from Aurora's bed,   135
Away from light steals home my heavy son   136
And private in his chamber pens himself,
Shuts up his windows, locks fair daylight out,
And makes himself an artificial night.
Black and portentous must this humor prove   *140*
Unless good counsel may the cause remove.

BENVOLIO
My noble uncle, do you know the cause?

MONTAGUE
I neither know it nor can learn of him.

BENVOLIO
Have you importuned him by any means?

MONTAGUE
Both by myself and many other friends;
But he, his own affections' counselor,
Is to himself – I will not say how true –
But to himself so secret and so close,
So far from sounding and discovery,   149
As is the bud bit with an envious worm   *150*
Ere he can spread his sweet leaves to the air

---

126 *most sought . . . found* i.e., desired solitude   **128** *humor* mood   **135** *Aurora* the goddess of dawn   **136** *heavy* melancholy   **149** *sounding* being measured (as water depth is measured with a plummet line)

Or dedicate his beauty to the sun.
Could we but learn from whence his sorrows grow,
We would as willingly give cure as know.
    Enter Romeo.
BENVOLIO
See, where he comes. So please you step aside,
I'll know his grievance, or be much denied.
MONTAGUE
I would thou wert so happy by thy stay
158 To hear true shrift. Come, madam, let's away.
                              Exeunt [Montague and his Wife].
BENVOLIO
159 Good morrow, cousin.
ROMEO   Is the day so young?
BENVOLIO
160 But new struck nine.
ROMEO   Ay me! sad hours seem long.
Was that my father that went hence so fast?
BENVOLIO
It was. What sadness lengthens Romeo's hours?
ROMEO
Not having that which having makes them short.
BENVOLIO   In love?
ROMEO   Out –
BENVOLIO   Of love?
ROMEO
Out of her favor where I am in love.
BENVOLIO
168 Alas that love, so gentle in his view,
169 Should be so tyrannous and rough in proof!
ROMEO
170 Alas that love, whose view is muffled still,
Should without eyes see pathways to his will!

---

158 *shrift* confession   159 *morrow* morning; *cousin* kinsman   168 *view* appearance   169 *in proof* in being experienced   170 *love* Cupid; *view* sight; *muffled* blindfolded

Where shall we dine? O me! What fray was here?
Yet tell me not, for I have heard it all.
Here's much to do with hate, but more with love.   174
Why then, O brawling love, O loving hate,
O anything, of nothing first create!
O heavy lightness, serious vanity,
Misshapen chaos of well-seeming forms,
Feather of lead, bright smoke, cold fire, sick health,
Still-waking sleep, that is not what it is!   180
This love feel I, that feel no love in this.
Dost thou not laugh?   182

BENVOLIO   No, coz, I rather weep.

ROMEO
Good heart, at what?

BENVOLIO   At thy good heart's oppression.

ROMEO
Why, such is love's transgression.
Griefs of mine own lie heavy in my breast,   185
Which thou wilt propagate, to have it prest
With more of thine. This love that thou hast shown
Doth add more grief to too much of mine own.
Love is a smoke made with the fume of sighs;
Being purged, a fire sparkling in lovers' eyes;   190
Being vexed, a sea nourished with loving tears.
What is it else? A madness most discreet,
A choking gall, and a preserving sweet.
Farewell, my coz.

BENVOLIO   Soft! I will go along.
An if you leave me so, you do me wrong.

ROMEO
Tut! I have lost myself; I am not here;   196
This is not Romeo, he's some other where.

174–81 *Here's ... this* (the rhetorical name for such paradoxes is oxymoron;
cf. III.2.73–85)   182 *coz* cousin   185 *Griefs ... own* your sorrow for my
grief grieves me further to have caused you sorrow   196 *lost* (so both Q2 and
Q1, but the emendation "left" has been cogently suggested)

BENVOLIO

198   Tell me in sadness, who is that you love?

ROMEO

What, shall I groan and tell thee?

BENVOLIO   Groan? Why, no;

200   But sadly tell me who.

ROMEO

Bid a sick man in sadness make his will.

Ah, word ill urged to one that is so ill!

In sadness, cousin, I do love a woman.

BENVOLIO

I aimed so near when I supposed you loved.

ROMEO

A right good markman. And she's fair I love.

BENVOLIO

206   A right fair mark, fair coz, is soonest hit.

ROMEO

Well, in that hit you miss. She'll not be hit

208   With Cupid's arrow. She hath Dian's wit,

209   And, in strong proof of chastity well armed,

210   From Love's weak childish bow she lives unharmed.

211   She will not stay the siege of loving terms,

Nor bide th' encounter of assailing eyes,

Nor ope her lap to saint-seducing gold.

O, she is rich in beauty; only poor

215   That, when she dies, with beauty dies her store.

BENVOLIO

216   Then she hath sworn that she will still live chaste?

ROMEO

217   She hath, and in that sparing makes huge waste;

For beauty, starved with her severity,

---

198 *in sadness* seriously **206** *fair mark* bright clean target **208** *Dian* Diana, virgin goddess of chastity and huntress **209** *proof* armor **210** *unharmed* (from Q1; Q2 reads "uncharmed," perhaps correctly) **211–12** *She . . . eyes* i.e., she gives me no chance to woo her **215** *with . . . store* she will leave no children to perpetuate her beauty **216** *still* always **217** *sparing* miserliness

Cuts beauty off from all posterity.
She is too fair, too wise, wisely too fair,   *220*
To merit bliss by making me despair.   221
She hath forsworn to love, and in that vow
Do I live dead that live to tell it now.

BENVOLIO
Be ruled by me; forget to think of her.

ROMEO
O, teach me how I should forget to think!

BENVOLIO
By giving liberty unto thine eyes.
Examine other beauties.

ROMEO   'Tis the way
To call hers, exquisite, in question more.   228
These happy masks that kiss fair ladies' brows,
Being black puts us in mind they hide the fair.   *230*
He that is strucken blind cannot forget
The precious treasure of his eyesight lost.
Show me a mistress that is passing fair,   233
What doth her beauty serve but as a note
Where I may read who passed that passing fair?
Farewell. Thou canst not teach me to forget.

BENVOLIO
I'll pay that doctrine, or else die in debt.   *Exeunt.*   237
                          *

∾ **I.2** *Enter Capulet, County Paris, and [Peter, Capulet's
servant].*

CAPULET
But Montague is bound as well as I,   1

---

221 *bliss* heaven **228** *in question* to my mind **233** *passing* surpassingly
237 *pay that doctrine* convince you otherwise
  I.2 s.d. *County* count; *Peter* (the role was played by Will Kemp, the
Clown of the company; the s.d. here reads "the Clowne" in Q2) **1** *bound*
under bond (to keep the peace)

In penalty alike; and 'tis not hard, I think,
For men so old as we to keep the peace.

PARIS

4   Of honorable reckoning are you both,
And pity 'tis you lived at odds so long.
But now, my lord, what say you to my suit?

CAPULET

But saying o'er what I have said before:

8   My child is yet a stranger in the world,
She hath not seen the change of fourteen years;

10   Let two more summers wither in their pride
Ere we may think her ripe to be a bride.

PARIS

Younger than she are happy mothers made.

CAPULET

13   And too soon marred are those so early made.
14   Earth hath swallowèd all my hopes but she;
15   She is the hopeful lady of my earth.
But woo her, gentle Paris, get her heart;
My will to her consent is but a part.

18   An she agree, within her scope of choice
19   Lies my consent and fair according voice.
20   This night I hold an old accustomed feast,
Whereto I have invited many a guest,
Such as I love; and you among the store,
One more, most welcome, makes my number more.
At my poor house look to behold this night

25   Earth-treading stars that make dark heaven light.
Such comfort as do lusty young men feel

27   When well-appareled April on the heel
Of limping winter treads, even such delight

---

4 *reckoning* reputation 8 *world* world of society 13 *too soon . . . made* (a proverb) 14 *hopes* children 15 *hopeful . . . earth* my hope for posterity and heir to my land 18 *scope* range 19 *according* harmoniously agreeing 20 *old accustomed* by custom of long standing 25 *Earth-treading stars* mortal stars – i.e., maidens 27 *April* (Venus's month, the season of lovemaking)

Among fresh fennel buds shall you this night   29
Inherit at my house. Hear all, all see,   30
And like her most whose merit most shall be;
Which, on more view of many, mine, being one,   32
May stand in number, though in reck'ning none.
Come, go with me.   34
   [To Peter, giving him a paper]
                Go, sirrah, trudge about
Through fair Verona; find those persons out
Whose names are written there, and to them say,
My house and welcome on their pleasure stay.
                    Exit [with Paris].
PETER   Find them out whose names are written here? It is
written that the shoemaker should meddle with his
yard and the tailor with his last, the fisher with his pen-   40
cil and the painter with his nets; but I am sent to find
those persons whose names are here writ, and can never
find what names the writing person hath here writ. I   43
must to the learned. In good time!   44
   Enter Benvolio and Romeo.

BENVOLIO

Tut, man, one fire burns out another's burning;   45
   One pain is lessened by another's anguish;   46
Turn giddy, and be holp by backward turning;   47
   One desperate grief cures with another's languish.

---

29 *fennel* a flowering herb supposed to awake sexual desire (but Q1 reads
"femelle"– i.e., "female"– and may be the right reading)   **32–33** *Which . . .
none* my daughter will be numerically counted among those present, but
possibly not among those you would wish to marry after seeing them all (cf.
the common saying "One is no number")   **34** *sirrah* (a usual form of address
to servants)   **40–41** *yard, last, pencil, nets* (occupational tools humorously
reversed; since "yard" and "pencil" often mean "penis," there is probably a
joke about masturbation here)   **43** *find* find out (since I cannot read)   **44**
In good time help comes just when I need it   **45** *one . . . burning* (proverb
used often by Shakespeare)   **46** *another's anguish* anguish from another pain
47 *Turn . . . turning* when giddy from whirling around, be helped by revers-
ing direction

49   Take thou some new infection to thy eye,
50   And the rank poison of the old will die.

ROMEO
     Your plantain leaf is excellent for that.

BENVOLIO
     For what, I pray thee?

ROMEO   For your broken shin.

BENVOLIO
     Why, Romeo, art thou mad?

ROMEO
54   Not mad, but bound more than a madman is;
     Shut up in prison, kept without my food,
56   Whipped and tormented and – God-den, good fellow.

PETER   God gi' god-den. I pray, sir, can you read?

ROMEO
     Ay, mine own fortune in my misery.

59 PETER   Perhaps you have learned it without book. But
60   I pray, can you read anything you see?

ROMEO
     Ay, if I know the letters and the language.

62 PETER   Ye say honestly. Rest you merry.

ROMEO   Stay, fellow; I can read.
        He reads the letter.
     "Signor Martino and his wife and daughters;
     County Anselme and his beauteous sisters;
     The lady widow of Vitruvio;
     Signor Placentio and his lovely nieces;
     Mercutio and his brother Valentine;
     Mine uncle Capulet, his wife, and daughters;
70   My fair niece Rosaline and Livia;
     Signor Valentio and his cousin Tybalt;

---

49 *infection* (figuratively used, but taken literally by Romeo) 54–56
bound . . . tormented (customary treatment of madmen) 56 *God-den* good
evening (used after 12 noon; cf. II.4.108) 59 *without book* by heart 62
Rest you merry good-bye (Peter gives up)

Lucio and the lively Helena."
A fair assembly. Whither should they come?
PETER   Up.
ROMEO   Whither?
PETER   To supper to our house.
ROMEO   Whose house?
PETER   My master's.
ROMEO
    Indeed I should have asked you that before.
PETER   Now I'll tell you without asking. My master is the   *80*
    great rich Capulet; and if you be not of the house of
    Montagues, I pray come and crush a cup of wine. Rest   *82*
    you merry.   *[Exit.]*
BENVOLIO
    At this same ancient feast of Capulet's
    Sups the fair Rosaline whom thou so loves,
    With all the admirèd beauties of Verona.
    Go thither, and with unattainted eye   *87*
    Compare her face with some that I shall show,
    And I will make thee think thy swan a crow.
ROMEO
    When the devout religion of mine eye   *90*
        Maintains such falsehood, then turn tears to fires;
    And these, who, often drowned, could never die,   *92*
        Transparent heretics, be burnt for liars!
    One fairer than my love? The all-seeing sun
    Ne'er saw her match since first the world begun.
BENVOLIO
    Tut! you saw her fair, none else being by,
    Herself poised with herself in either eye;
    But in that crystal scales let there be weighed   *98*
    Your lady's love against some other maid

---

82 *crush* drink   **87** *unattainted* unprejudiced   **92** *these* these eyes; *drowned*
i.e., in tears   **98** *crystal scales* (Romeo's two eyes are compared to the two
ends of a pair of balances)

100 That I will show you shining at this feast,
101 And she shall scant show well that now seems best.
ROMEO
I'll go along, no such sight to be shown,
But to rejoice in splendor of my own. *[Exeunt.]*

*

∽ **I.3** *Enter Capulet's Wife, and Nurse.*

CAPULET'S WIFE
Nurse, where's my daughter? Call her forth to me.
NURSE
Now, by my maidenhead at twelve year old,
3 I bade her come. What, lamb! what, ladybird!
God forbid. Where's this girl? What, Juliet!
Enter Juliet.
JULIET
How now? Who calls?
NURSE   Your mother.
JULIET   Madam, I am here.
What is your will?
CAPULET'S WIFE
7 This is the matter – nurse, give leave awhile,
We must talk in secret. Nurse, come back again;
9 I have remembered me, thou's hear our counsel.
10 Thou knowest my daughter's of a pretty age.
NURSE
Faith, I can tell her age unto an hour.
CAPULET'S WIFE
She's not fourteen.
NURSE   I'll lay fourteen of my teeth –
13 And yet, to my teen be it spoken, I have but four –

---

101 *scant* scarcely
 I.3 In Capulet's house **3** *ladybird* (1) darling, (2) prostitute (hence perhaps
"God forbid") **7** *give leave* leave us **9** *thou's* thou shalt **13** *teen* sorrow

She's not fourteen. How long is it now
To Lammastide?   15
CAPULET'S WIFE   A fortnight and odd days.
NURSE
  Even or odd, of all days in the year,
  Come Lammas Eve at night shall she be fourteen.
  Susan and she (God rest all Christian souls!)   18
  Were of an age. Well, Susan is with God;
  She was too good for me. But, as I said,   20
  On Lammas Eve at night shall she be fourteen;
  That shall she, marry; I remember it well.
  'Tis since the earthquake now eleven years;
  And she was weaned (I never shall forget it),
  Of all the days of the year, upon that day,
  For I had then laid wormwood to my dug,   26
  Sitting in the sun under the dovehouse wall.
  My lord and you were then at Mantua.
  Nay, I do bear a brain. But, as I said,   29
  When it did taste the wormwood on the nipple   30
  Of my dug and felt it bitter, pretty fool,
  To see it tetchy and fall out with the dug!   32
  Shake, quoth the dovehouse! 'Twas no need, I trow,   33
  To bid me trudge.   34
  And since that time it is eleven years,
  For then she could stand high-lone; nay, by th' rood,   36
  She could have run and waddled all about;
  For even the day before, she broke her brow,
  And then my husband (God be with his soul!
  A was a merry man) took up the child.   40
  "Yea," quoth he, "dost thou fall upon thy face?
  Thou wilt fall backward when thou hast more wit;   42

---

15 *Lammastide* August 1   18 *Susan* (the nurse's dead daughter)   26 *wormwood* (a bitter-tasting herb used to wean the child from the breast, "dug")
29 *bear a brain* keep my powers of memory   32 *tetchy* fretful   33 *Shake . . .
dovehouse* i.e., the dovehouse shook from the earthquake(?); *trow* believe   34
trudge run away   36 *high-lone* alone; *rood* cross   40 *A* he   42 *fall backward*
(ready for sex)

43   Wilt thou not, Jule?" and, by my holidam,
      The pretty wretch left crying and said "Ay."
      To see now how a jest shall come about!
      I warrant, an I should live a thousand years,
      I never should forget it. "Wilt thou not, Jule?" quoth he,
48   And, pretty fool, it stinted and said "Ay."

CAPULET'S WIFE
      Enough of this. I pray thee hold thy peace.

NURSE
50   Yes, madam. Yet I cannot choose but laugh
      To think it should leave crying and say "Ay."
52   And yet, I warrant, it had upon it brow
53   A bump as big as a young cock'rel's stone –
      A perilous knock – and it cried bitterly.
      "Yea," quoth my husband, "fall'st upon thy face?
      Thou wilt fall backward when thou comest to age;
      Wilt thou not, Jule?" It stinted and said "Ay."

JULIET
58   And stint thou too, I pray thee, nurse, say I.

NURSE
      Peace, I have done. God mark thee to his grace!
60   Thou wast the prettiest babe that e'er I nursed.
      An I might live to see thee married once,
      I have my wish.

CAPULET'S WIFE
      Marry, that "marry" is the very theme
      I came to talk of. Tell me, daughter Juliet,
      How stands your disposition to be married?

JULIET
      It is an honor that I dream not of.

NURSE
      An honor? Were not I thine only nurse,
      I would say thou hadst sucked wisdom from thy teat.

---

43 *holidam* halidom, holy relic   48 *stinted* stopped   52 *it brow* its brow   53
stone testicle   58 *say I* (a pun on "ay" and "I"; cf. III.2.45–50)

CAPULET'S WIFE
  Well, think of marriage now. Younger than you,
  Here in Verona, ladies of esteem,   70
  Are made already mothers. By my count,
  I was your mother much upon these years   72
  That you are now a maid. Thus then in brief:
  The valiant Paris seeks you for his love.
NURSE
  A man, young lady, lady, such a man
  As all the world – why he's a man of wax.   76
CAPULET'S WIFE
  Verona's summer hath not such a flower.
NURSE
  Nay, he's a flower, in faith – a very flower.
CAPULET'S WIFE
  What say you? Can you love the gentleman?
  This night you shall behold him at our feast.   80
  Read o'er the volume of young Paris' face,
  And find delight writ there with beauty's pen;
  Examine every married lineament,   83
  And see how one another lends content;
  And what obscured in this fair volume lies   85
  Find written in the margent of his eyes.   86
  This precious book of love, this unbound lover,   87
  To beautify him only lacks a cover.   88
  The fish lives in the sea, and 'tis much pride   89
  For fair without the fair within to hide.   90
  That book in many's eyes doth share the glory,

---

72 *much . . . years* at much the same age (Juliet's mother is claiming to be twenty-eight; she *may* be exaggerating her youth)   76 *a man of wax* handsome, as a wax model   83 *married lineament* harmonious feature   85 *what . . . lies* i.e., his concealed inner qualities of character   86 *margent* marginal gloss   87 *unbound* (like a book and because still unmarried)   88 *a cover* i.e., a wife   89–94 *The fish . . . no less* i.e., as the sea enfolds the fish and the cover enfolds the book, so you shall enfold Paris (in your arms), enhancing your good qualities by sharing his

That in gold clasps locks in the golden story;
So shall you share all that he doth possess,
By having him making yourself no less.

NURSE

95   No less? Nay, bigger! Women grow by men.

CAPULET'S WIFE

Speak briefly, can you like of Paris' love?

JULIET

I'll look to like, if looking liking move;
98   But no more deep will I endart mine eye
Than your consent gives strength to make it fly.

Enter Peter.

100 PETER   Madam, the guests are come, supper served up,
101 you called, my young lady asked for, the nurse cursed
in the pantry, and everything in extremity. I must
hence to wait. I beseech you follow straight.

CAPULET'S WIFE

We follow thee.   *[Exit Peter.]*
              Juliet, the county stays.

NURSE

Go, girl, seek happy nights to happy days.   *Exeunt.*

                            ✳

∾ **I.4** *Enter Romeo, Mercutio, Benvolio, with five or six
other Maskers; Torchbearers.*

ROMEO

1   What, shall this speech be spoke for our excuse?
Or shall we on without apology?

BENVOLIO

3   The date is out of such prolixity.

---

95 *bigger* i.e., through pregnancy **98** *endart mine eye* shoot my eye glance
(as an arrow; cf. III.2.47)   **101–2** *cursed in the pantry* i.e., the other servants
swear because the nurse is not helping
  I.4   1 *this speech* (Romeo has prepared a set speech, such as customarily
introduced visiting maskers) **3** *The date . . . prolixity* such superfluous
speeches are now out of fashion

We'll have no Cupid hoodwinked with a scarf,   4
Bearing a Tartar's painted bow of lath,   5
Scaring the ladies like a crowkeeper;   6
[Nor no without-book prologue, faintly spoke   7
After the prompter, for our entrance;]
But, let them measure us by what they will,
We'll measure them a measure and be gone.   10

ROMEO
Give me a torch. I am not for this ambling.
Being but heavy, I will bear the light.   12

MERCUTIO
Nay, gentle Romeo, we must have you dance.

ROMEO
Not I, believe me. You have dancing shoes
With nimble soles; I have a soul of lead
So stakes me to the ground I cannot move.

MERCUTIO
You are a lover. Borrow Cupid's wings
And soar with them above a common bound.   18

ROMEO
I am too sore enpiercèd with his shaft
To soar with his light feathers; and so bound   *20*
I cannot bound a pitch above dull woe.   21
Under love's heavy burden do I sink.

MERCUTIO
And, to sink in it, should you burden love –
Too great oppression for a tender thing.

ROMEO
Is love a tender thing? It is too rough,
Too rude, too boist'rous, and it pricks like thorn.

4–5 (the prologue for the maskers will not be a boy dressed as Cupid)   4
hoodwinked blindfolded   5 *Tartar's . . . lath* (the Tartar's bow, used from
horseback, was much shorter and more curved than the English longbow
and hence more like Cupid's); *lath* flimsy piece of wood   6 *crowkeeper* scare-
crow   7–8 (added from Q1)   7 *without-book* memorized   10 *measure . . .
measure* dance one dance   12 *heavy* sad, hence "weighted down"   18 *bound*
(1) limit, (2) a leap, required in some dances   21 *pitch* height (falconry)

MERCUTIO

If love be rough with you, be rough with love,
28 Prick love for pricking, and you beat love down.
29 Give me a case to put my visage in.
30 A visor for a visor! What care I
31 What curious eye doth quote deformities?
32 Here are the beetle brows shall blush for me.

BENVOLIO

Come, knock and enter; and no sooner in
34 But every man betake him to his legs.

ROMEO

A torch for me! Let wantons light of heart
36 Tickle the senseless rushes with their heels;
37 For I am proverbed with a grandsire phrase,
38 I'll be a candle holder and look on;
39 The game was ne'er so fair, and I am done.

MERCUTIO

40 Tut! dun's the mouse, the constable's own word!
41 If thou art Dun, we'll draw thee from the mire
42 Of this sir-reverence love, wherein thou stickest
43 Up to the ears. Come, we burn daylight, ho!

ROMEO

Nay, that's not so.

---

28 *Prick . . . pricking* (Mercutio puns on "screw love for screwing you about" or "stimulate love to be ready for sex"; "beat love down" suggests "lose an erection")   29 *case* mask (also "vagina")   30 *A visor . . . visor* a mask for a face ugly enough to be itself a mask   31 *quote* note   32 *beetle brows* beetling eyebrows (of the mask)   34 *betake . . . legs* join the dance   36 *rushes* (used as floor coverings)   37 *grandsire phrase* old saying   38 *candle holder* i.e., non-participant ("A good candle holder is a good gamester" was proverbial, meaning "You can't lose if you only watch")   39 *The game . . . done* best quit a game at the height of enjoyment (proverbial; cf. I.5.120)   40 *dun's the mouse* be quiet as a mouse (proverbial); *constable's own word* the constable warns his men to be quiet   41 *Dun* (stock name for a horse); *mire* (alluding to a winter game, "Dun is in the mire," in which the players lifted a heavy log representing a horse caught in the mud; Romeo is a stick-in-the-mud)   42 *sir-reverence* filthy (literally "save-your-reverence," a euphemism for "dung"; Mercutio apologizes for using the filthy word "love")   43 *burn daylight* waste time (proverbial)

MERCUTIO   I mean, sir, in delay
  We waste our lights in vain, like lamps by day.
  Take our good meaning, for our judgment sits
  Five times in that ere once in our five wits.   47
ROMEO
  And we mean well in going to this masque,
  But 'tis no wit to go.   49
MERCUTIO   Why, may one ask?
ROMEO
  I dreamt a dream tonight.   50
MERCUTIO   And so did I.
ROMEO
  Well, what was yours?
MERCUTIO   That dreamers often lie.
ROMEO
  In bed asleep, while they do dream things true.
MERCUTIO
  O, then I see Queen Mab hath been with you.   53
  She is the fairies' midwife, and she comes
  In shape no bigger than an agate stone   55
  On the forefinger of an alderman,
  Drawn with a team of little atomi   57
  Over men's noses as they lie asleep;
  Her wagon spokes made of long spinners' legs,   59
  The cover, of the wings of grasshoppers;   60
  Her traces, of the smallest spiderweb;   61
  Her collars, of the moonshine's wat'ry beams;
  Her whip, of cricket's bone; the lash, of film;   63
  Her wagoner, a small gray-coated gnat,   64

---

47 *five wits* mental faculties; common sense (the perceptive power common
to all five physical senses), fantasy, imagination, judgment (reason), memory
49 *no wit* not intelligent   53 *Mab* (a Celtic folk name for the fairy queen);
you (Q1 adds a line for Benvolio here: "Queen Mab, what's she?")   55 *agate
stone* jewel carved with figures and set in a ring   57 *atomi* tiny creatures,
specks of dust   59 *spinners* spiders   61–62 *traces, collars* parts of the harness
63 *film* gossamer thread   64 *wagoner* charioteer

65 Not half so big as a round little worm
   Pricked from the lazy finger of a maid;
   Her chariot is an empty hazelnut,
   Made by the joiner squirrel or old grub,
   Time out o' mind the fairies' coachmakers.
70 And in this state she gallops night by night
   Through lovers' brains, and then they dream of love;
   O'er courtiers' knees, that dream on curtsies straight;
   O'er lawyers' fingers, who straight dream on fees;
   O'er ladies' lips, who straight on kisses dream,
   Which oft the angry Mab with blisters plagues,
76 Because their breaths with sweetmeats tainted are.
   Sometime she gallops o'er a courtier's nose,
78 And then dreams he of smelling out a suit;
79 And sometime comes she with a tithe-pig's tail
80 Tickling a parson's nose as a lies asleep,
81 Then dreams he of another benefice.
   Sometime she driveth o'er a soldier's neck,
   And then dreams he of cutting foreign throats,
   Of breaches, ambuscadoes, Spanish blades,
85 Of healths five fathom deep; and then anon
   Drums in his ear, at which he starts and wakes,
   And being thus frighted, swears a prayer or two
   And sleeps again. This is that very Mab
   That plaits the manes of horses in the night
90 And bakes the elflocks in foul sluttish hairs,
   Which once untangled much misfortune bodes.
92 This is the hag, when maids lie on their backs,

65–66 *worm . . . maid* (alluding to the proverbial saying that worms breed in idle fingers)   **70** *state* pomp   **76** *with sweetmeats* i.e., as a result of eating sweetmeats   **78** *smelling . . . suit* discovering a petitioner who will pay for his influence with government officials   **79** *tithe-pig* a pig paid to the parish priest as a tithe (tenth) of his parishioner's livestock   **81** *another benefice* an additional "living" in the church   **85** *healths . . . deep* drinking toasts from glasses thirty feet deep   **90** *elflocks* knots of tangled hair, supposedly the work of elves who avenged its untangling   **92** *hag* night hag, or nightmare

That presses them and learns them first to bear,   93
Making them women of good carriage.   94
This is she –
ROMEO   Peace, peace, Mercutio, peace!
Thou talk'st of nothing.   96
MERCUTIO   True, I talk of dreams;
Which are the children of an idle brain,
Begot of nothing but vain fantasy;   98
Which is as thin of substance as the air,
And more inconstant than the wind, who woos   100
Even now the frozen bosom of the North
And, being angered, puffs away from thence,
Turning his side to the dew-dropping South.
BENVOLIO
This wind you talk of blows us from ourselves.
Supper is done, and we shall come too late.
ROMEO
I fear, too early; for my mind misgives
Some consequence, yet hanging in the stars,   107
Shall bitterly begin his fearful date
With this night's revels and expire the term
Of a despisèd life, closed in my breast,   110
By some vile forfeit of untimely death.
But he that hath the steerage of my course   112
Direct my sail! On, lusty gentlemen!   113
BENVOLIO   Strike, drum.
                    They march about the stage and [exeunt].
                                    *

---

93 *to bear* (1) to put up with the man's weight during intercourse, (2) to have
children   **94** *good carriage* (1) good at sex, (2) good at having children, (3)
good deportment   **96** *nothing* no tangible thing   **98** *vain fantasy* empty
imagination   **107** *consequence* future chain of events; *hanging* (in astrology,
future events are said to "hang" – *dependere* – from the stars)   **112** *he* God
113 *sail* voyage

❧ **I.5** *Servingmen come forth with napkins.*

1 FIRST SERVINGMAN   Where's Potpan, that he helps not to
2 take away? He shift a trencher! he scrape a trencher!
3 SECOND SERVINGMAN   When good manners shall lie all
in one or two men's hands, and they unwashed too, 'tis
a foul thing.
6 FIRST SERVINGMAN   Away with the joint stools, remove
7 the court cupboard, look to the plate. Good thou, save
8 me a piece of marchpane and, as thou loves me, let the
9 porter let in Susan Grindstone and Nell. *[Exit second*
10 *Servingman.]* Anthony, and Potpan!
[Enter Anthony and Potpan.]
11 ANTHONY   Ay, boy, ready.
FIRST SERVINGMAN   You are looked for and called for,
asked for and sought for, in the great chamber.
POTPAN   We cannot be here and there too. Cheerly, boys!
15 Be brisk awhile, and the longer liver take all.

[Exeunt.]
Enter [Capulet, his Wife, his Cousin, Juliet, Tybalt,
Tybalt's Page, Nurse, and] all the Guests and
Gentlewomen to the Maskers [including Romeo,
Benvolio, and Mercutio].

I.5 Within Capulet's house **s.d.** (Q2 adds "Enter Romeo," altered in folio to
"Enter Servant." It is not certain that the maskers leave the stage at this
point; "marching about" itself sometimes signaled a change in locale.)   **1, 3**
First Servingman, Second Servingman (designated "Servingman," "1. Servingman" in Q2; 1. Servingman is probably Peter)   **2** *take away* clear the table;
trencher wooden platter   **3–5** *When . . . thing* (a complaint that household
decorum, "good manners," is sustained by too few, and too dirty, servants)
6 *joint stools* stools made by a joiner   **7** *court cupboard* sideboard; *plate* sil-
verware   **8** *marchpane* marzipan, made with sugar and almonds   **9**
Susan . . . Nell (girls evidently invited for a servants' party in the kitchen after
the banquet)   **11,14** *Anthony, Potpan* (designated "2." and "3." in Q2, but
Anthony and Potpan have now arrived)   **15** *longer . . . all* i.e., the spoils to
the survivor (proverbial, but often used in contexts like the above, advocat-
ing enjoyment of life)   **15 s.d.** Exeunt . . . *Potpan* (at least one servingman
is onstage for Romeo to question at l. 42; he and the others probably come and
go during the dancing – e.g., bringing on lights after Capulet's order at l. 27)

CAPULET
    Welcome, gentlemen! Ladies that have their toes
    Unplagued with corns will walk a bout with you.   17
    Ah ha, my mistresses, which of you all
    Will now deny to dance? She that makes dainty,   19
    She I'll swear hath corns. Am I come near ye now?   20
    Welcome, gentlemen! I have seen the day
    That I have worn a visor and could tell
    A whispering tale in a fair lady's ear,
    Such as would please. 'Tis gone, 'tis gone, 'tis gone!
    You are welcome, gentlemen! Come, musicians, play.
      Music plays, and they dance.
    A hall, a hall! give room! and foot it, girls.   26
    More light, you knaves! and turn the tables up,
    And quench the fire, the room is grown too hot.
    Ah, sirrah, this unlooked-for sport comes well.   29
    Nay, sit, nay, sit, good cousin Capulet,   30
    For you and I are past our dancing days.
    How long is't now since last yourself and I
    Were in a mask?
CAPULET'S COUSIN By'r Lady, thirty years.   34
CAPULET
    What, man? 'Tis not so much, 'tis not so much;
    'Tis since the nuptial of Lucentio,
    Come Pentecost as quickly as it will,
    Some five-and-twenty years, and then we masked.
CAPULET'S COUSIN
    'Tis more, 'tis more. His son is elder, sir;
    His son is thirty.   40
CAPULET   Will you tell me that?
    His son was but a ward two years ago.   41

---

17 *walk a bout* dance a turn **19** *makes dainty* pretends to hesitate **26** *A hall* clear the hall for dancing **29** *unlooked-for sport* (a dance was not originally planned) **34** *thirty years* (indicating Capulet's advanced age) **41** *His son . . . ago* it seems only two years since his son was a minor

ROMEO   *[To a Servingman]*
  What lady's that, which doth enrich the hand
  Of yonder knight?
44 SERVINGMAN   I know not, sir.
ROMEO
  O, she doth teach the torches to burn bright!
  It seems she hangs upon the cheek of night
  As a rich jewel in an Ethiop's ear –
  Beauty too rich for use, for earth too dear!
49 So shows a snowy dove trooping with crows
50 As yonder lady o'er her fellows shows.
  The measure done, I'll watch her place of stand
52 And, touching hers, make blessèd my rude hand.
  Did my heart love till now? Forswear it, sight!
  For I ne'er saw true beauty till this night.
TYBALT
  This, by his voice, should be a Montague.
    [To his Page]
  Fetch me my rapier, boy. What, dares the slave
57 Come hither, covered with an antic face,
58 To fleer and scorn at our solemnity?
  Now, by the stock and honor of my kin,
60 To strike him dead I hold it not a sin.
CAPULET
  Why, how now, kinsman? Wherefore storm you so?
TYBALT
  Uncle, this is a Montague, our foe,
  A villain, that is hither come in spite
  To scorn at our solemnity this night.
CAPULET
  Young Romeo is it?

---

44 (the servingman may be too busy to be bothered to answer Romeo prop-
erly, but if he does not recognize Juliet he is not likely to be a regular mem-
ber of the Capulet household and hence not *First Servingman*)   49 *with
crows* (cf. I.2.89)   52 *rude* rough   57 *antic face* comic mask   58 *fleer* mock;
solemnity dignified feast

TYBALT   'Tis he, that villain Romeo.
CAPULET
  Content thee, gentle coz, let him alone.
  A bears him like a portly gentleman,   67
  And, to say truth, Verona brags of him
  To be a virtuous and well-governed youth.
  I would not for the wealth of all this town   70
  Here in my house do him disparagement.
  Therefore be patient, take no note of him.
  It is my will, the which if thou respect,
  Show a fair presence and put off these frowns,
  An ill-beseeming semblance for a feast.
TYBALT
  It fits when such a villain is a guest.
  I'll not endure him.
CAPULET   He shall be endured.
  What, goodman boy! I say he shall. Go to!   78
  Am I the master here, or you? Go to!
  You'll not endure him, God shall mend my soul!   80
  You'll make a mutiny among my guests!   81
  You will set cock-a-hoop, you'll be the man!   82
TYBALT
  Why, uncle, 'tis a shame.
CAPULET   Go to, go to!
  You are a saucy boy. Is't so, indeed?
  This trick may chance to scathe you. I know what.   85
  You must contrary me! Marry, 'tis time –   86
  Well said, my hearts! – You are a princox – go!   87
  Be quiet, or – More light, more light! – For shame!
  I'll make you quiet; what! – Cheerly, my hearts!

---

67 *portly* well-mannered   78 *goodman* yeoman (hence an insult to Tybalt, who is a gentleman)   80 *God . . . soul* (an expression of impatience)   81 *mutiny* violent disturbance   82 *set cock-a-hoop* act without restraint; *be the man* play the big man   85 *scathe* injure; *what* what I'm doing   86 *'tis time* it's time you learned your place   87 *said* done; *my hearts* (addressed to the dancers); *princox* saucy boy

TYBALT

90   Patience perforce with willful choler meeting
     Makes my flesh tremble in their different greeting.
     I will withdraw; but this intrusion shall,
     Now seeming sweet, convert to bitt'rest gall.   *Exit.*

ROMEO   *[To Juliet]*

94   If I profane with my unworthiest hand
95   This holy shrine, the gentle sin is this:
96   My lips, two blushing pilgrims, ready stand
        To smooth that rough touch with a tender kiss.

JULIET

98   Good pilgrim, you do wrong your hand too much,
        Which mannerly devotion shows in this;
100 For saints have hands that pilgrims' hands do touch,
101   And palm to palm is holy palmers' kiss.

ROMEO

     Have not saints lips, and holy palmers too?

JULIET

     Ay, pilgrim, lips that they must use in prayer.

ROMEO

104 O, then, dear saint, let lips do what hands do!
        They pray; grant thou, lest faith turn to despair.

JULIET

106 Saints do not move, though grant for prayers' sake.

ROMEO

     Then move not while my prayer's effect I take.
     Thus from my lips, by thine my sin is purged.
        [Kisses her.]

---

90 *Patience perforce* enforced self-restraint; *choler* anger   **94–101** (these lines form a sonnet and the first quatrain of another)   **95** *shrine* i.e., Juliet's hand; *this* the kiss he proposes (which would be "gentle," unlike the meeting of her soft hand and his rough one)   **96** *pilgrims* (so called because pilgrims visit shrines)   **98–101** *Good . . . kiss* your touch is not rough, to heal it with a kiss is unnecessary, a handclasp is sufficient greeting   **101** *palmers* religious pilgrims   **104** *do what hands do* i.e., press each other (in a kiss)   **106** *move* take the initiative; *grant* respond (to prayer through intercession)

JULIET
    Then have my lips the sin that they have took.

ROMEO
  Sin from my lips? O trespass sweetly urged!   *110*
    Give me my sin again.   111
    [Kisses her.]

JULIET   You kiss by th' book.

NURSE
  Madam, your mother craves a word with you.
    [Juliet goes to talk with her mother.]

ROMEO
  What is her mother?

NURSE   Marry, bachelor,
  Her mother is the lady of the house,
  And a good lady, and a wise and virtuous.
  I nursed her daughter that you talked withal.   116
  I tell you, he that can lay hold of her
  Shall have the chinks.   118

ROMEO   Is she a Capulet?
  O dear account! my life is my foe's debt.   119

BENVOLIO
  Away, be gone; the sport is at the best.   120

ROMEO
  Ay, so I fear; the more is my unrest.

CAPULET
  Nay, gentlemen, prepare not to be gone;
  We have a trifling foolish banquet towards.   123
  Is it e'en so? Why then, I thank you all.
  I thank you, honest gentlemen. Good night.
  More torches here! Come on then, let's to bed.
  Ah, sirrah, by my fay, it waxes late;   127
  I'll to my rest.
      [Everyone except Juliet and Nurse starts to leave.]

---

111 *by th' book* expertly   **116** *withal* with   **118** *chinks* money   **119** *my foe's debt* owed to my foe   **120** *Away . . . best* (cf. I.4.39)   **123** *banquet* light refreshments; *towards* just ready   **127** *fay* faith

JULIET
    Come hither, nurse. What is yond gentleman?
NURSE
130   The son and heir of old Tiberio.
JULIET
    What's he that now is going out of door?
NURSE
    Marry, that, I think, be young Petruccio.
JULIET
    What's he that follows there, that would not dance?
NURSE
    I know not.
JULIET
    Go ask his name. – If he be marrièd,
    My grave is like to be my wedding bed.
NURSE
    His name is Romeo, and a Montague,
    The only son of your great enemy.
JULIET
    My only love, sprung from my only hate!
140   Too early seen unknown, and known too late!
141   Prodigious birth of love it is to me
    That I must love a loathèd enemy.
NURSE
143   What's tis? what's tis?
JULIET   A rhyme I learnt even now
144   Of one I danced withal.
        One calls within, "Juliet."
NURSE   Anon, anon!
    Come, let's away; the strangers all are gone.   *Exeunt.*

                            ✳

---

141 *Prodigious* monstrous   **143** *tis* this   **144** *Anon* i.e., we are coming right
away

∾ **II. Cho.** *[Enter] Chorus.*

CHORUS
  Now old desire doth in his deathbed lie,   1
    And young affection gapes to be his heir;   2
  That fair for which love groaned for and would die,
    With tender Juliet matched, is now not fair.
  Now Romeo is beloved and loves again,
    Alike bewitchèd by the charm of looks;
  But to his foe supposed he must complain,   7
    And she steal love's sweet bait from fearful hooks.   8
  Being held a foe, he may not have access
    To breathe such vows as lovers use to swear,   10
  And she as much in love, her means much less
    To meet her new belovèd anywhere;
  But passion lends them power, time means, to meet,
  Temp'ring extremities with extreme sweet.   *[Exit.]*   14

                    ✳

∾ **II.1** *Enter Romeo alone.*

ROMEO
  Can I go forward when my heart is here?   1
  Turn back, dull earth, and find thy center out.   2
    [Romeo retires.] Enter Benvolio with Mercutio.
BENVOLIO
  Romeo! my cousin Romeo! Romeo!
MERCUTIO   He is wise,
  And, on my life, hath stol'n him home to bed.

II.Cho. 1–14 (another sonnet; cf. Prologue and I.5.94–111) **1** *old desire*
i.e., Romeo's love of Rosaline **2** *young affection* new love; *gapes* opens his
mouth hungrily **7** *complain* make a lover's plaints **8** *steal . . . hooks* (a popular conceit: the lover "fishes" for his beloved; for Juliet to be "caught" is dangerous because of the family feud) **10** *use* are accustomed **14** *Temp'ring
extremities* mitigating their plight

  II.1 Outside Capulet's walled orchard **1** *my heart is here* (the Neo-
Platonic fancy that the heart or soul of the lover dwells in the beloved) **2**
earth i.e., my body; *center* i.e., my heart or soul, Juliet

BENVOLIO

　　He ran this way and leapt this orchard wall.

6　　Call, good Mercutio.

MERCUTIO　　　　　　　　　Nay, I'll conjure too.

7　　Romeo! humors! madman! passion! lover!

　　Appear thou in the likeness of a sigh;

　　Speak but one rhyme, and I am satisfied!

10　　Cry but "Ay me!", pronounce but "love" and "dove";

11　　Speak to my gossip Venus one fair word,

12　　One nickname for her purblind son and heir

13　　Young Abraham Cupid, he that shot so trim

14　　When King Cophetua loved the beggar maid!

　　He heareth not, he stirreth not, he moveth not;

16　　The ape is dead, and I must conjure him.

　　I conjure thee by Rosaline's bright eyes,

　　By her high forehead and her scarlet lip,

　　By her fine foot, straight leg, and quivering thigh,

20　　And the demesnes that there adjacent lie,

　　That in thy likeness thou appear to us!

BENVOLIO

　　An if he hear thee, thou wilt anger him.

MERCUTIO

　　This cannot anger him. 'Twould anger him

24　　To raise a spirit in his mistress' circle

　　Of some strange nature, letting it there stand

　　Till she had laid it and conjured it down.

　　That were some spite; my invocation

---

6 *Nay . . . too* (printed as part of preceding speech in Q2)　7 *humors* whims
11 *gossip* female crony　12 *purblind* dim-sighted　13 *Young Abraham*
youthful, yet patriarchal (Cupid, or Love, was both the youngest and the
oldest of the gods)　14 *King Cophetua . . . beggar maid* (from an old ballad;
he made her his queen)　16 *ape* (term of endearment; cf. modern "monkey")
20 *demesnes* domains (i.e., her genitals)　24 *circle* the conjurer's circle in
which an evoked spirit supposedly appears　24–26 (as well as the image of
magic, Mercutio also means "for the penis of some stranger to become erect
in his mistress's vagina, letting it stay erect there until she had brought it to
ejaculate and made it lose its erection")

Is fair and honest: in his mistress' name,
I conjure only but to raise up him.   29

BENVOLIO

Come, he hath hid himself among these trees   30
To be consorted with the humorous night.   31
Blind is his love and best befits the dark.

MERCUTIO

If love be blind, love cannot hit the mark.
Now will he sit under a medlar tree   34
And wish his mistress were that kind of fruit
As maids call medlars when they laugh alone.
O, Romeo, that she were, O that she were
An open-arse and thou a popp'ring pear!   38
Romeo, good night. I'll to my truckle bed;   39
This field bed is too cold for me to sleep.   40
Come, shall we go?

BENVOLIO   Go then, for 'tis in vain
To seek him here that means not to be found.

Exit [with Mercutio].

*

❧ II.2

ROMEO   *[Coming forward]*
He jests at scars that never felt a wound.

---

29 *raise up him* give him an erection   31 (1) *humorous* (1) damp, (2) capri-
cious   34 *medlar* (1) a small, brown apple, (2) a slang term for the vulva   38
open-arse (another name for the medlar, making the sexual pun explicit);
popp'ring pear (1) a phallic-shaped pear, (2) an erect penis   39 *truckle bed* a
low bed stored under an ordinary bed   40 *field bed* a soldier's portable bed,
lying in the open air

II.2 (Though a new scene is conventionally marked here, the action is
continuous. Romeo has not left the stage, but the fictional locale has now
moved inside the Capulet orchard. Juliet enters on the area above the main
stage.)   **s.d.** (No entrance is marked for Juliet in any early edition. She
might appear here, or Romeo might only see a light at this point, with Juliet
entering at l.10)

[Enter Juliet above at a window.]
But soft! What light through yonder window breaks?
It is the east, and Juliet is the sun!
4 Arise, fair sun, and kill the envious moon,
Who is already sick and pale with grief
6 That thou her maid art far more fair than she.
Be not her maid, since she is envious.
8 Her vestal livery is but sick and green,
And none but fools do wear it. Cast it off.
10 It is my lady; O, it is my love!
O that she knew she were!
She speaks, yet she says nothing. What of that?
Her eye discourses; I will answer it.
I am too bold; 'tis not to me she speaks.
Two of the fairest stars in all the heaven,
Having some business, do entreat her eyes
17 To twinkle in their spheres till they return.
18 What if her eyes were there, they in her head?
The brightness of her cheek would shame those stars
20 As daylight doth a lamp; her eyes in heaven
Would through the airy region stream so bright
That birds would sing and think it were not night.
See how she leans her cheek upon her hand!
O that I were a glove upon that hand,
That I might touch that cheek!
JULIET   Ay me!
ROMEO   She speaks.
O, speak again, bright angel! for thou art
As glorious to this night, being o'er my head,
As is a wingèd messenger of heaven
29 Unto the white-upturnèd wond'ring eyes

---

4 *kill* make invisible by more intense light   6 *her maid* (Diana, moon goddess, was patroness of virgins)   8 *vestal livery* the uniform of Diana's votaries;
sick and green anemic, the pallor of moonlight   17 *spheres* orbits (the con-
centric shells that carried the heavenly bodies in Ptolemaic astronomy)   18
there i.e., in the stars' spheres   29 *white-upturnèd* (the whites show when the
eyes are turned upward)

Of mortals that fall back to gaze on him   *30*
When he bestrides the lazy-pacing clouds
And sails upon the bosom of the air.

JULIET
O Romeo, Romeo! wherefore art thou Romeo?   *33*
Deny thy father and refuse thy name;
Or, if thou wilt not, be but sworn my love,
And I'll no longer be a Capulet.

ROMEO   *[Aside]*
Shall I hear more, or shall I speak at this?

JULIET
'Tis but thy name that is my enemy.
Thou art thyself, though not a Montague.   *39*
What's Montague? It is nor hand, nor foot,   *40*
Nor arm, nor face, nor any other part
Belonging to a man. O, be some other name!
What's in a name? That which we call a rose
By any other word would smell as sweet.   *44*
So Romeo would, were he not Romeo called,
Retain that dear perfection which he owes   *46*
Without that title. Romeo, doff thy name;
And for thy name, which is no part of thee,
Take all myself.

ROMEO   I take thee at thy word.
Call me but love, and I'll be new baptized.   *50*
Henceforth I never will be Romeo.

JULIET
What man art thou that, thus bescreened in night,
So stumblest on my counsel?

ROMEO   By a name
I know not how to tell thee who I am.
My name, dear saint, is hateful to myself,
Because it is an enemy to thee.
Had I it written, I would tear the word.

---

33 *wherefore* why   **39** *though not* even if you were not   **44** *word* (Q1 reads
"name")   **46** *owes* owns

JULIET

My ears have yet not drunk a hundred words
Of thy tongue's uttering, yet I know the sound.

60   Art thou not Romeo, and a Montague?

ROMEO

61   Neither, fair maid, if either thee dislike.

JULIET

How camest thou hither, tell me, and wherefore?
The orchard walls are high and hard to climb,
And the place death, considering who thou art,
If any of my kinsmen find thee here.

ROMEO

66   With love's light wings did I o'erperch these walls;
For stony limits cannot hold love out,
And what love can do, that dares love attempt.
Therefore thy kinsmen are no stop to me.

JULIET

70   If they do see thee, they will murder thee.

ROMEO

Alack, there lies more peril in thine eye
Than twenty of their swords! Look thou but sweet,

73   And I am proof against their enmity.

JULIET

I would not for the world they saw thee here.

ROMEO

I have night's cloak to hide me from their eyes;

76   And but thou love me, let them find me here.
My life were better ended by their hate

78   Than death proroguèd, wanting of thy love.

JULIET

By whose direction found'st thou out this place?

ROMEO

80   By love, that first did prompt me to inquire.
He lent me counsel, and I lent him eyes.

---

61 *thee dislike* displeases you   66 *o'erperch* fly over   73 *proof* armored   76
but unless   78 *proroguèd* postponed; *wanting of* lacking

I am no pilot; yet, wert thou as far
As that vast shore washed with the farthest sea,   83
I should adventure for such merchandise.   84

JULIET

Thou knowest the mask of night is on my face;
Else would a maiden blush bepaint my cheek
For that which thou hast heard me speak tonight.
Fain would I dwell on form – fain, fain deny
What I have spoke; but farewell compliment!   89
Dost thou love me? I know thou wilt say "Ay,"   90
And I will take thy word. Yet, if thou swear'st,
Thou mayst prove false. At lovers' perjuries,
They say Jove laughs. O gentle Romeo,
If thou dost love, pronounce it faithfully.
Or if thou thinkest I am too quickly won,
I'll frown, and be perverse, and say thee nay,
So thou wilt woo; but else, not for the world.
In truth, fair Montague, I am too fond,
And therefore thou mayst think my havior light;   99
But trust me, gentleman, I'll prove more true   100
Than those that have more cunning to be strange.   101
I should have been more strange, I must confess,
But that thou overheard'st, ere I was ware,   103
My true-love passion. Therefore pardon me,
And not impute this yielding to light love,
Which the dark night hath so discoverèd.   106

ROMEO

Lady, by yonder blessèd moon I vow,
That tips with silver all these fruit-tree tops –

JULIET

O, swear not by the moon, th' inconstant moon,
That monthly changes in her circled orb,   110
Lest that thy love prove likewise variable.

---

83 *farthest sea* the Pacific   84 *adventure* risk a voyage   89 *compliment* etiquette   99 *havior* behavior; *light* wanton   101 *strange* aloof, distant   103
ware aware of you   106 *discoverèd* revealed

ROMEO
What shall I swear by?

JULIET   Do not swear at all,
Or if thou wilt, swear by thy gracious self,
Which is the god of my idolatry,
And I'll believe thee.

ROMEO   If my heart's dear love –

JULIET
Well, do not swear. Although I joy in thee,
I have no joy of this contract tonight.
It is too rash, too unadvised, too sudden;
Too like the lightning, which doth cease to be
120   Ere one can say "It lightens." Sweet, good night!
This bud of love, by summer's ripening breath,
May prove a beauteous flow'r when next we meet.
Good night, good night! As sweet repose and rest
Come to thy heart as that within my breast!

ROMEO
O, wilt thou leave me so unsatisfied?

JULIET
What satisfaction canst thou have tonight?

ROMEO
Th' exchange of thy love's faithful vow for mine.

JULIET
I gave thee mine before thou didst request it;
And yet I would it were to give again.

ROMEO
130   Wouldst thou withdraw it? For what purpose, love?

JULIET
131   But to be frank and give it thee again.
And yet I wish but for the thing I have.
My bounty is as boundless as the sea,
My love as deep; the more I give to thee,
135   The more I have, for both are infinite.

---

131 *frank* generous   135 *The more I have* (scholastic theologians debated
how love could be given away and yet the giver have more than before)

[Nurse calls within.]
I hear some noise within. Dear love, adieu!
Anon, good nurse! Sweet Montague, be true.
Stay but a little, I will come again.   *[Exit.]*
ROMEO
O blessèd, blessèd night! I am afeard,
Being in night, all this is but a dream,   *140*
Too flattering-sweet to be substantial.
    [Enter Juliet above.]
JULIET
Three words, dear Romeo, and good night indeed.
If that thy bent of love be honorable,   *143*
Thy purpose marriage, send me word tomorrow,
By one that I'll procure to come to thee,
Where and what time thou wilt perform the rite;
And all my fortunes at thy foot I'll lay
And follow thee my lord throughout the world.
NURSE   *[Within]* Madam!
JULIET
I come, anon. – But if thou meanest not well,   *150*
I do beseech thee –
NURSE   *[Within]*
Madam!   *152*
JULIET   By and by I come. –
To cease thy strife and leave me to my grief.   *153*
Tomorrow will I send.
ROMEO   So thrive my soul –
JULIET
A thousand times good night!   *[Exit.]*
ROMEO
A thousand times the worse, to want thy light!
Love goes toward love as schoolboys from their books;
But love from love, toward school with heavy looks.
    Enter Juliet [above] again.

---

143 *bent* purpose   **152** *By and by* immediately   **153** *strife* striving (editors
often follow Q4 and emend to "suit")

JULIET

Hist! Romeo, hist! O for a falconer's voice
160   To lure this tassel-gentle back again!
161   Bondage is hoarse and may not speak aloud,
162   Else would I tear the cave where Echo lies
And make her airy tongue more hoarse than mine
With repetition of my Romeo's name. Romeo!

ROMEO

165   It is my soul that calls upon my name.
How silver-sweet sound lovers' tongues by night,
167   Like softest music to attending ears!

JULIET

168   Romeo!

ROMEO   My nyas?

JULIET   What o'clock tomorrow
Shall I send to thee?

ROMEO   By the hour of nine.

JULIET

170   I will not fail. 'Tis twenty years till then.
I have forgot why I did call thee back.

ROMEO

Let me stand here till thou remember it.

JULIET

I shall forget, to have thee still stand there,
Rememb'ring how I love thy company.

ROMEO

And I'll still stay, to have thee still forget,
Forgetting any other home but this.

JULIET

'Tis almost morning. I would have thee gone –
178   And yet no farther than a wanton's bird,

---

160 *tassel-gentle* tercel-gentle, or male goshawk (a falcon for princes)   161
Bondage is hoarse (one confined can only whisper loudly)   162 *Echo* (in
Ovid's *Metamorphoses* Echo, rejected by Narcissus, pined away in a cave until
only her voice remained)   165 *my soul* (cf. II.1.1 and note)   167 *attending*
paying attention   168 *nyas* nestling hawk   178 *wanton* spoiled child

That lets it hop a little from her hand,
Like a poor prisoner in his twisted gyves,   180
And with a silken thread plucks it back again,
So loving-jealous of his liberty.

ROMEO
I would I were thy bird.

JULIET   Sweet, so would I.
Yet I should kill thee with much cherishing.   184
Good night, good night! Parting is such sweet sorrow
That I shall say good night till it be morrow.   *[Exit.]*   186

ROMEO
Sleep dwell upon thine eyes, peace in thy breast!   187
Would I were sleep and peace, so sweet to rest!
Hence will I to my ghostly sire's close cell,   189
His help to crave and my dear hap to tell.   *[Exit.]*   190

*

∾ **II.3** *Enter Friar [Laurence] alone, with a basket.*

FRIAR
The gray-eyed morn smiles on the frowning night,
Check'ring the eastern clouds with streaks of light;
And fleckled darkness like a drunkard reels   3
From forth day's path and Titan's fiery wheels.   4
Now, ere the sun advance his burning eye
The day to cheer and night's dank dew to dry,
I must upfill this osier cage of ours   7
With baleful weeds and precious-juicèd flowers.   8

---

180 *gyves* fetters   184 *cherishing* caressing   186 *morrow* morning   **187–89**
(In Q2 the speech prefix "Juliet" is mistakenly placed before the first of these
lines, and they are followed by four lines that are nearly identical with those
at II.3.1–4. Perhaps Shakespeare decided to let the friar announce the dawn
in place of Romeo, and the canceled lines in the manuscript were printed in
error.)   189 *ghostly* spiritual   190 *dear hap* good luck
 II.3 Before Friar Laurence's cell   3 *fleckled* spotted, dappled   4 *Titan's
fiery wheels* the sun's chariot wheels (Helios, the sun god, was a Titan)   7
osier cage willow basket   8 *baleful* harmful

The earth that's nature's mother is her tomb.
10   What is her burying grave, that is her womb;
And from her womb children of divers kind
We sucking on her natural bosom find,
Many for many virtues excellent,
None but for some, and yet all different.
15   O, mickle is the powerful grace that lies
In plants, herbs, stones, and their true qualities.
For naught so vile that on the earth doth live
But to the earth some special good doth give;
Nor aught so good but, strained from that fair use,
20   Revolts from true birth, stumbling on abuse.
Virtue itself turns vice, being misapplied,
22   And vice sometime's by action dignified.

    Enter Romeo.

Within the infant rind of this weak flower
Poison hath residence, and medicine power;
25   For this, being smelt, with that part cheers each part;
Being tasted, slays all senses with the heart.
27   Two such opposèd kings encamp them still
In man as well as herbs – grace and rude will;
And where the worser is predominant,
30   Full soon the canker death eats up that plant.

ROMEO
31   Good morrow, father.

FRIAR   Benedicite!
What early tongue so sweet saluteth me?
33   Young son, it argues a distempered head
So soon to bid good morrow to thy bed.
Care keeps his watch in every old man's eye,
And where care lodges, sleep will never lie;
37   But where unbruisèd youth with unstuffed brain

---

15 *mickle* much   20 *true birth* is true nature   22 *dignified* made worthy; **s.d.**
(this entrance seems premature, but cf. entrance of Nurse at III.3.78)   25–
26 *being . . . heart* i.e., being smelt, stimulates; being tasted, kills   27 *still* always   30 *canker* the worm in the bud   31 *morrow* morning; *Benedicite* bless
you   33 *distempered* disturbed   37 *unstuffed* carefree

Doth couch his limbs, there golden sleep doth reign.
Therefore thy earliness doth me assure
Thou art uproused with some distemp'rature;   40
Or if not so, then here I hit it right –
Our Romeo hath not been in bed tonight.
ROMEO
That last is true – the sweeter rest was mine.
FRIAR
God pardon sin! Wast thou with Rosaline?
ROMEO
With Rosaline, my ghostly father? No.
I have forgot that name and that name's woe.
FRIAR
That's my good son! But where hast thou been then?
ROMEO
I'll tell thee ere thou ask it me again.
I have been feasting with mine enemy,
Where on a sudden one hath wounded me   50
That's by me wounded. Both our remedies
Within thy help and holy physic lies.   52
I bear no hatred, blessèd man, for, lo,
My intercession likewise steads my foe.   54
FRIAR
Be plain, good son, and homely in thy drift.   55
Riddling confession finds but riddling shrift.   56
ROMEO
Then plainly know my heart's dear love is set
On the fair daughter of rich Capulet;
As mine on hers, so hers is set on mine,
And all combined, save what thou must combine   60
By holy marriage. When, and where, and how
We met, we wooed, and made exchange of vow,
I'll tell thee as we pass; but this I pray,   63
That thou consent to marry us today.

---

52 *physic* medicine 54 *intercession* request; *steads* benefits 55 *homely* simple; *drift* explanation 56 *shrift* absolution 63 *pass* go along

FRIAR
    Holy Saint Francis! What a change is here!
    Is Rosaline, that thou didst love so dear,
    So soon forsaken? Young men's love then lies
    Not truly in their hearts, but in their eyes.
    Jesu Maria! What a deal of brine
70   Hath washed thy sallow cheeks for Rosaline!
    How much salt water thrown away in waste
72   To season love, that of it doth not taste!
    The sun not yet thy sighs from heaven clears,
    Thy old groans ring yet in mine ancient ears.
    Lo, here upon thy cheek the stain doth sit
    Of an old tear that is not washed off yet.
    If e'er thou wast thyself, and these woes thine,
    Thou and these woes were all for Rosaline.
    And art thou changed? Pronounce this sentence then:
80   Women may fall when there's no strength in men.
ROMEO
    Thou chid'st me oft for loving Rosaline.
FRIAR
    For doting, not for loving, pupil mine.
ROMEO
    And bad'st me bury love.
FRIAR   Not in a grave
    To lay one in, another out to have.
ROMEO
    I pray thee chide not. Her I love now
86   Doth grace for grace and love for love allow.
    The other did not so.
FRIAR   O, she knew well
88   Thy love did read by rote, that could not spell.
    But come, young waverer, come go with me.
90   In one respect I'll thy assistant be;

---

72 *season* preserve, flavor; *doth not taste* i.e., now has no savor   80 *strength* constancy   86 *grace* favor   88 *by rote . . . spell* like a child, who cannot read, pretending to read by learning by heart

For this alliance may so happy prove
To turn your households' rancor to pure love.

ROMEO

O, let us hence! I stand on sudden haste.   93

FRIAR

Wisely and slow. They stumble that run fast.   *Exeunt.*

*

∾ **II.4** *Enter Benvolio and Mercutio.*

MERCUTIO

Where the devil should this Romeo be?
Came he not home tonight?   2

BENVOLIO

Not to his father's. I spoke with his man.

MERCUTIO

Why, that same pale hard-hearted wench, that Rosaline,
Torments him so that he will sure run mad.

BENVOLIO

Tybalt, the kinsman to old Capulet,
Hath sent a letter to his father's house.

MERCUTIO   A challenge, on my life.

BENVOLIO   Romeo will answer it.   9

MERCUTIO   Any man that can write may answer a letter. 10

BENVOLIO   Nay, he will answer the letter's master, how
he dares, being dared.

MERCUTIO   Alas, poor Romeo, he is already dead, stabbed
with a white wench's black eye, run through the ear with
a love song, the very pin of his heart cleft with the blind 15
bow-boy's butt shaft; and is he a man to encounter 16
Tybalt?

BENVOLIO   Why, what is Tybalt?

---

93 *on* in need of
  II.4 A public place in Verona **2** *tonight* last night **9** *answer it* accept the
challenge **15** *pin* peg in the center of a target, a bull's-eye **16** *bow-boy's
butt shaft* Cupid's arrow (a butt shaft was an unbarbed arrow, suitable for
children and hence for Cupid)

19 MERCUTIO   More than Prince of Cats, I can tell you. O,
20   he's the courageous captain of compliments. He fights
21   as you sing prick song – keeps time, distance, and pro-
22   portion; he rests his minim rests, one, two, and the
23   third in your bosom! the very butcher of a silk button,
24   a duelist, a duelist! a gentleman of the very first house,
25   of the first and second cause. Ah, the immortal passado!
26   the punto reverso! the hai!

BENVOLIO   The what?

28 MERCUTIO   The pox of such antic, lisping, affecting
29   phantasims – these new tuners of accent! "By Jesu, a
30   very good blade! a very tall man! a very good whore!"
31   Why, is not this a lamentable thing, grandsire, that we
   should be thus afflicted with these strange flies, these
33   fashionmongers, these pardon-me's, who stand so
34   much on the new form that they cannot sit at ease on
35   the old bench? O, their bones, their bones!

   Enter Romeo.

BENVOLIO   Here comes Romeo! here comes Romeo!

37 MERCUTIO   Without his roe, like a dried herring. O
38   flesh, flesh, how art thou fishified! Now is he for the
39   numbers that Petrarch flowed in. Laura, to his lady, was

---

19 *Prince of Cats* (Tybalt, or Tybert, is the cat's name in medieval stories of
Reynard the Fox)   20 *captain of compliments* master of dueling   21 *sing
prick song* sing written music (i.e., accurately)   22 *minim rests* shortest rests
(in the old musical notation)   23 *third* third rapier thrust; *button* i.e., on his
opponent's shirt   24 *first house* finest fencing school   25 *first and second
cause* causes for a challenge (in the duelist's code); *passado* lunge   26 *punto
reverso* back-handed stroke; *hai* home thrust (from "hai," "I have it" – a new
term to Benvolio)   28 *The pox of* a plague on; *antic* grotesque   29 *phantasims* foppish coxcombs; *new tuners of accent* people who add new words to
their language   30 *tall* brave   31 *grandsire* good sir   33 *pardon-me's* i.e.,
sticklers for etiquette; *stand* insist (pun on "sit," l. 34)   34 *form* (1) fashion,
(2) school bench   35 *old bench* i.e., native manners and learning; *bones* (pun
on French *bons,* "goods")   37 *Without his roe* (1) without his roe deer (dear),
(2) sighing melancholically "oh me" (from "Roe-me-oh"), (3) looking thin,
sexually exhausted (without his seed, "roe")   38 *fishified* turned cold-
blooded (with no sexual heat)   39 *numbers* verses; *Petrarch* Italian Renais-
sance poet who wrote love poems to Laura

a kitchen wench (marry, she had a better love to *40*
berhyme her), Dido a dowdy, Cleopatra a gypsy, Helen *41*
and Hero hildings and harlots, Thisbe a gray eye or so, *42*
but not to the purpose. Signor Romeo, *bonjour!* *43*
There's a French salutation to your French slop. You *44*
gave us the counterfeit fairly last night. *45*

ROMEO   Good morrow to you both. What counterfeit
did I give you?

MERCUTIO   The slip, sir, the slip. Can you not conceive? *48*

ROMEO   Pardon, good Mercutio. My business was great,
and in such a case as mine a man may strain courtesy. *50*

MERCUTIO   That's as much as to say, such a case as yours *51*
constrains a man to bow in the hams. *52*

ROMEO   Meaning, to curtsy.

MERCUTIO   Thou has most kindly hit it. *54*

ROMEO   A most courteous exposition.

MERCUTIO   Nay, I am the very pink of courtesy.

ROMEO   Pink for flower. *57*

MERCUTIO   Right.

ROMEO   Why, then is my pump well-flowered. *59*

MERCUTIO   Sure wit, follow me this jest now till thou *60*
hast worn out thy pump, that, when the single sole of it
is worn, the jest may remain, after the wearing, solely *62*
singular.

---

41 *Dido* queen of Carthage who was loved and abandoned by Aeneas; *dowdy*
homely; *Cleopatra* queen of Egypt who was loved by Julius Caesar and Mark
Antony; *gypsy* Egyptian, whore; *Helen* Helen of Troy   **42** *Hero* loved by Le-
ander; *hildings* worthless creatures; *Thisbe* (Pyramus and Thisbe were young
lovers whose story resembles that of Romeo and Juliet)   **43** *not to the purpose*
not worth mentioning; *bon jour* good day   **44** *slop* trousers   **45** *fairly* effectively   **48** *slip* (1) escape, (2) counterfeit coin   **50** *courtesy* good manners
51 *such . . . . yours* (1) your condition, (2) the vagina you have been having sex
with   **52** *bow in the hams* (1) make a bow, (2) show the effects of venereal
disease   **54** *kindly hit it* interpreted it in a good sense (where Mercutio had
intended a double meaning)   **57** *flower* ("flower of courtesy" was the usual
complimentary form; cf. II.5.43)   **59** *pump* shoe; *well-flowered* (because
pinked, or punched, with an ornamental design)   **62–63** *solely singular*
uniquely remarkable

64 ROMEO   O single-soled jest, solely singular for the singleness!

MERCUTIO   Come between us, good Benvolio! My wits
faint.

68 ROMEO   Swits and spurs, swits and spurs! or I'll cry a
match.

70 MERCUTIO   Nay, if our wits run the wild-goose chase, I
am done; for thou hast more of the wild goose in one of

72 thy wits than, I am sure, I have in my whole five. Was I
with you there for the goose?

74 ROMEO   Thou wast never with me for anything when
thou wast not there for the goose.

MERCUTIO   I will bite thee by the ear for that jest.

77 ROMEO   Nay, good goose, bite not!

78 MERCUTIO   Thy wit is a very bitter sweeting; it is a most
sharp sauce.

80 ROMEO   And is it not, then, well served in to a sweet
goose?

82 MERCUTIO   O, here's a wit of cheveril, that stretches from
83 an inch narrow to an ell broad!

ROMEO   I stretch it out for that word "broad," which,
85 added to the goose, proves thee far and wide a broad
goose.

MERCUTIO   Why, is not this better now than groaning
for love? Now art thou sociable, now art thou Romeo;
now art thou what thou art, by art as well as by nature.
90 For this driveling love is like a great natural that runs
91 lolling up and down to hide his bauble in a hole.

---

64 *single-soled* weak   64–65 *singleness* weakness   68 *Swits and spurs* switches and spurs – i.e., keep your horse (wit) running fast   68–69 *cry a match* claim victory   70 *wild-goose chase* cross-country horse race of "follow the leader"   72–73 *Was . . . goose* was I accurate in calling you a goose   74–75 *Thou . . . goose* you were never in my company for any purpose when you weren't looking for a prostitute (goose)   77 *good . . . not* spare me (proverbial)   78 *bitter sweeting* a tart species of apple   80 *sweet* tasty, tender   82 *cheveril* kidskin, easily stretched   83 *ell* forty-five inches (English measure)   85–86 *broad goose* a complete fool   90 *natural* idiot   91 *bauble* jester's wand, penis

BENVOLIO   Stop there, stop there!

MERCUTIO   Thou desirest me to stop in my tale against   93
the hair.

BENVOLIO   Thou wouldst else have made thy tale large.   95

MERCUTIO   O, thou art deceived! I would have made it
short; for I was come to the whole depth of my tale,
and meant indeed to occupy the argument no longer.   98

ROMEO   Here's goodly gear!   99
  Enter Nurse and her Man [Peter].
A sail, a sail!   100

MERCUTIO   Two, two! a shirt and a smock.   101

NURSE   Peter!

PETER   Anon.

NURSE   My fan, Peter.

MERCUTIO   Good Peter, to hide her face; for her fan's the
fairer face.

NURSE   God ye good morrow, gentlemen.

MERCUTIO   God ye good-den, fair gentlewoman.

NURSE   Is it good-den?   109

MERCUTIO   'Tis no less, I tell ye; for the bawdy hand of   *110*
the dial is now upon the prick of noon.   111

NURSE   Out upon you! What a man are you!

ROMEO   One, gentlewoman, that God hath made for
himself to mar.

NURSE   By my troth, it is well said. "For himself to mar,"
quoth a? Gentlemen, can any of you tell me where I   116
may find the young Romeo?

93–94 *stop . . . hair* (1) stop my story against my wish, (2) stuff my penis,
"tail," in up to my pubic hair (the punning continues with "large"
[= "erect"], "short" [= "limp"], "come to the whole depth of my tale" [= "in-
sert to the whole length of my penis"], etc.)   95 *large* broad, indecent   98
occupy the argument pursue the subject   99 *gear* stuff (a comment on either
Mercutio's jokes or the nurse's arrival)   100–1 (Q1 gives l. 100 to Mercutio
and l. 101 to Benvolio)   101 *shirt, smock* male and female garments   109 *Is
it good-den* is it already afternoon   111 *prick* (1) indented point on a clock
face or sundial, (2) phallus   116 *quoth a* said he

ROMEO   I can tell you; but young Romeo will be older
when you have found him than he was when you
120   sought him. I am the youngest of that name, for fault
of a worse.

NURSE   You say well.

123   MERCUTIO   Yea, is the worst well? Very well took, i' faith!
wisely, wisely.

125   NURSE   If you be he, sir, I desire some confidence with
you.

127   BENVOLIO   She will indite him to some supper.

128   MERCUTIO   A bawd, a bawd, a bawd! So ho!

ROMEO   What hast thou found?

130   MERCUTIO   No hare, sir; unless a hare, sir, in a lenten pie,
131   that is something stale and hoar ere it be spent.
[He walks by them and sings.]
An old hare hoar,
And an old hare hoar,
Is very good meat in Lent;
But a hare that is hoar
136   Is too much for a score
When it hoars ere it be spent.
Romeo, will you come to your father's? We'll to dinner
thither.

140   ROMEO   I will follow you.

141   MERCUTIO   Farewell, ancient lady. Farewell *[Sings.]*, lady,
lady, lady.   *Exeunt [Mercutio, Benvolio]*.

143   NURSE   I pray you, sir, what saucy merchant was this that
144   was so full of his ropery?

120–21 *for . . . worse* (parodying "for want of a better")   **123** *took* under-
stood   **125** *confidence* conference (malapropism)   **127** *indite* invite (an
ironic malapropism)   **128** *So ho* (hunter's cry on sighting game)   **130** *hare*
i.e., prostitute; *lenten pie* pie with no meat (i.e., without a penis), eaten during Lent   **131** *stale* (also a slang term for a prostitute); *hoar* gray with mold,
punning on "whore"; **s.d.** (from Q1)   **136** *Is . . . score* is not worth paying
for ("score" = "bill")   **141–42** *lady, lady, lady* (Mercutio mockingly sings the
refrain from "Chaste Susanna," a ballad about a chaste woman)   **143** *merchant* fellow   **144** *ropery* vulgar jesting

ROMEO A gentleman, nurse, that loves to hear himself talk and will speak more in a minute than he will stand to in a month.

NURSE An a speak anything against me, I'll take him down, an a were lustier than he is, and twenty such Jacks; and if I cannot, I'll find those that shall. Scurvy knave! I am none of his flirt-gills; I am none of his skeans-mates. *[To Peter]* And thou must stand by too, and suffer every knave to use me at his pleasure! 148 150 151 152

PETER I saw no man use you at his pleasure. If I had, my weapon should quickly have been out, I warrant you. I dare draw as soon as another man, if I see occasion in a good quarrel, and the law on my side. 154 155

NURSE Now, afore God, I am so vexed that every part about me quivers. Scurvy knave! Pray you, sir, a word; and, as I told you, my young lady bid me inquire you out. What she bid me say, I will keep to myself; but first let me tell ye, if ye should lead her into a fool's paradise, as they say, it were a very gross kind of behavior, as they say, for the gentlewoman is young, and therefore, if you should deal double with her, truly it were an ill thing to be offered to any gentlewoman, and very weak dealing. 160 162 166

ROMEO Nurse, commend me to thy lady and mistress. I protest unto thee – 168

NURSE Good heart, and i' faith I will tell her as much. Lord, Lord! she will be a joyful woman. 170

ROMEO What wilt thou tell her, nurse? Thou dost not mark me.

NURSE I will tell her, sir, that you do protest, which, as I take it, is a gentleman-like offer.

148–49 *take him down* cut him down to size (unintentionally [?] punning on "cause him to lose his erection") **150** *Jacks* cheeky guys **151** *flirt-gills* loose women **152** *skeans-mates* outlaws, gangster molls (a "skean" is a dagger) **154** *use* have sex with **155** *weapon* (1) dagger, (2) penis **162** *lead . . . paradise* seduce her (proverbial) **166** *weak* unmanly **168** *protest* (1) declare, (2) solemnly vow (Nurse hears the latter meaning)

ROMEO
  Bid her devise
  Some means to come to shrift this afternoon;
  And there she shall at Friar Laurence' cell
  Be shrived and married. Here is for thy pains.
  [Offering her money]
  NURSE   No, truly, sir; not a penny.
180 ROMEO   Go to! I say you shall.
  NURSE   This afternoon, sir? Well, she shall be there.
ROMEO
  And stay, good nurse, behind the abbey wall.
  Within this hour my man shall be with thee
184 And bring thee cords made like a tackled stair,
185 Which to the high topgallant of my joy
186 Must be my convoy in the secret night.
187 Farewell. Be trusty, and I'll quit thy pains.
  Farewell. Commend me to thy mistress.
NURSE
  Now God in heaven bless thee! Hark you, sir.
ROMEO
190 Why say'st thou, my dear nurse?
NURSE
  Is your man secret? Did you ne'er hear say,
  Two may keep counsel, putting one away?
ROMEO
  I warrant thee my man's as true as steel.
  NURSE   Well, sir, my mistress is the sweetest lady. Lord,
  Lord! when 'twas a little prating thing – O, there is a
196 nobleman in town, one Paris, that would fain lay knife
197 aboard; but she, good soul, had as lief see a toad, a very
  toad, as see him. I anger her sometimes, and tell her

---

184 *tackled stair* rope ladder   185 *topgallant* mast and sail above the main-
mast   186 *convoy* conveyance   187 *quit thy pains* reward your efforts
196–97 *lay knife aboard* i.e., partake of this dish (with a pun on "knife" as
"penis"), press his claim   197 *lief* willingly

that Paris is the properer man; but I'll warrant you,
when I say so, she looks as pale as any clout in the ver-   200
sal world. Doth not rosemary and Romeo begin both
with a letter?   202

ROMEO   Ay, nurse; what of that? Both with an R.

NURSE   Ah, mocker! that's the dog's name. R is for the –   204
no, I know it begins with some other letter – and she
hath the prettiest sententious of it, of you and rose-   206
mary, that it would do you good to hear it.

ROMEO   Commend me to thy lady.

NURSE   Ay, a thousand times. *[Exit Romeo.]* Peter!

PETER   Anon.   210

NURSE   Before, and apace.   211

                                        Exit [after Peter].

                            ✳

∾ **II.5**   *Enter Juliet.*

JULIET
   The clock struck nine when I did send the nurse;
   In half an hour she promised to return.
   Perchance she cannot meet him. That's not so.
   O, she is lame! Love's heralds should be thoughts,
   Which ten times faster glides than the sun's beams
   Driving back shadows over low'ring hills.
   Therefore do nimble-pinioned doves draw Love,   7
   And therefore hath the wind-swift Cupid wings.
   Now is the sun upon the highmost hill   9
   Of this day's journey, and from nine till twelve   10

---

200 *clout* cloth   **200–1** *versal* universal   **202** *with a* with the same   **204**
dog's name (*R* was called "the dog's letter," since the sound "r-r-r-r" supposedly resembles a dog's growl. The nurse thinks it an ugly sound.)   **206** *sen-*
tentious sentences   **211** *Before* (Q1 reads "Peter, take my fan and go before,"
probably recording comic stage business)
   II.5 At Capulet's house   **7** *nimble-pinioned* swift-winged; *doves* (Venus's
birds, who draw her chariot)   **9** *upon . . . hill* at the zenith

Is three long hours; yet she is not come.
Had she affections and warm youthful blood,
She would be as swift in motion as a ball;
14   My words would bandy her to my sweet love,
And his to me.
16   But old folks, many feign as they were dead –
Unwieldy, slow, heavy and pale as lead.
       Enter Nurse [and Peter].
O God, she comes! O honey nurse, what news?
Hast thou met with him? Send thy man away.

NURSE
20   Peter, stay at the gate.   *[Exit Peter.]*

JULIET
Now, good sweet nurse – O Lord, why lookest thou
   sad?
Though news be sad, yet tell them merrily;
If good, thou shamest the music of sweet news
By playing it to me with so sour a face.

NURSE
25   I am aweary, give me leave awhile.
26   Fie, how my bones ache! What a jaunce have I!

JULIET
I would thou hadst my bones, and I thy news.
Nay, come, I pray thee speak. Good, good nurse, speak.

NURSE
29   Jesu, what haste! Can you not stay awhile?
30   Do you not see that I am out of breath?

JULIET
How art thou out of breath when thou hast breath
To say to me that thou art out of breath?
The excuse that thou dost make in this delay
Is longer than the tale thou dost excuse.
Is thy news good or bad? Answer to that.

---

14 *bandy* toss   16 *old . . . dead* many persons speak figuratively of old folks
as being dead   25 *give me leave* let me alone   26 *jaunce* jolting   29 *stay* wait

Say either, and I'll stay the circumstance.   36
Let me be satisfied: is't good or bad?

NURSE   Well, you have made a simple choice; you know   38
not how to choose a man. Romeo? No, not he. Though
his face be better than any man's, yet his leg excels all   40
men's, and for a hand and a foot and a body, though
they be not to be talked on, yet they are past compare.
He is not the flower of courtesy but, I'll warrant him, as
gentle as a lamb. Go thy ways, wench; serve God.
What, have you dined at home?

JULIET
No, no. But all this did I know before.
What says he of our marriage? What of that?

NURSE
Lord, how my head aches! What a head have I!
It beats as it would fall in twenty pieces.
My back a t' other side – ah, my back, my back!   50
Beshrew your heart for sending me about   51
To catch my death with jauncing up and down!

JULIET
I' faith, I am sorry that thou art not well.
Sweet, sweet, sweet nurse, tell me, what says my love?

NURSE   Your love says, like an honest gentleman, and a
courteous, and a kind, and a handsome, and, I warrant,
a virtuous – Where is your mother?

JULIET
Where is my mother? Why, she is within.
Where should she be? How oddly thou repliest!
"Your love says, like an honest gentleman,   60
'Where is your mother?'"

NURSE   O God's Lady dear!
Are you so hot? Marry, come up, I trow.   62

---

36 *stay the circumstance* wait for details   38 *simple* foolish   50 *a* on   51
Beshrew shame on   62 *hot* impatient; *Marry come up* by the Virgin Mary,
take your comeuppance (penalty); *trow* trust

Is this the poultice for my aching bones?
Henceforward do your messages yourself.

JULIET

65   Here's such a coil! Come, what says Romeo?

NURSE

Have you got leave to go to shrift today?

JULIET

I have.

NURSE

Then hie you hence to Friar Laurence' cell;
There stays a husband to make you a wife.
70   Now comes the wanton blood up in your cheeks:
71   They'll be in scarlet straight at any news.
Hie you to church. I must another way,
To fetch a ladder, by the which your love
74   Must climb a bird's nest soon when it is dark.
I am the drudge, and toil in your delight;
76   But you shall bear the burden soon at night.
Go, I'll to dinner, hie you to the cell.

JULIET

Hie to high fortune! Honest nurse, farewell.   *Exeunt.*

                                  *

∾ **II.6** *Enter Friar [Laurence] and Romeo.*

FRIAR

So smile the heavens upon this holy act
That after-hours with sorrow chide us not!

ROMEO

Amen, amen! But come what sorrow can,
4   It cannot countervail the exchange of joy
That one short minute gives me in her sight.

---

65 *coil* fuss 71 *in scarlet* (Juliet blushes easily – cf. II.2.86; III.2.14); *straight*
straightway 74 *climb . . . nest* i.e., climb to Juliet's room 76 *the burden* (1)
the responsibility, (2) your lover's weight
II.6 At Friar Laurence's cell 4 *countervail* outweigh

Do thou but close our hands with holy words,
Then love-devouring death do what he dare –
It is enough I may but call her mine.

FRIAR

These violent delights have violent ends
And in their triumph die, like fire and powder,   10
Which, as they kiss, consume. The sweetest honey
Is loathsome in his own deliciousness   12
And in the taste confounds the appetite.
Therefore love moderately: long love doth so;
Too swift arrives as tardy as too slow.   15
    Enter Juliet.
Here comes the lady. O, so light a foot
Will ne'er wear out the everlasting flint.   17
A lover may bestride the gossamer   18
That idles in the wanton summer air,
And yet not fall; so light is vanity.   20

JULIET

Good even to my ghostly confessor.   21

FRIAR

Romeo shall thank thee, daughter, for us both.

JULIET

As much to him, else is his thanks too much.   23

ROMEO

Ah, Juliet, if the measure of thy joy
Be heaped like mine, and that thy skill be more   25
To blazon it, then sweeten with thy breath   26
This neighbor air, and let rich music's tongue
Unfold the imagined happiness that both
Receive in either by this dear encounter.

---

12 *Is loathsome* i.e., if eaten to excess 15 *Too . . . slow* (proverbial;
cf. II.3.94); **s.d.** (Q1 reads "Enter Juliet somewhat fast and embraceth
Romeo") 17 *wear . . . flint* (suggested by the proverb "In time small water
drops will wear away the stone") 18 *gossamer* spider's web 20 *vanity* tran-
sitory earthly love (cf. Ecclesiastes 9:9) 21 *ghostly* spiritual 23 *As much* the
same greeting 25 *that* if 26 *blazon* proclaim

JULIET

30   Conceit, more rich in matter than in words,
      Brags of his substance, not of ornament.
      They are but beggars that can count their worth;
33   But my true love is grown to such excess
      I cannot sum up sum of half my wealth.

FRIAR

      Come, come with me, and we will make short work,
      For, by your leaves, you shall not stay alone
      Till Holy Church incorporate two in one.   *[Exeunt.]*

                         ✳

∾ **III.1** *Enter Mercutio [, his Page], Benvolio, and Men.*

BENVOLIO

      I pray thee, good Mercutio, let's retire.
      The day is hot, the Capels are abroad,
      And, if we meet, we shall not scape a brawl,
      For now, these hot days, is the mad blood stirring.

MERCUTIO   Thou art like one of these fellows that, when
      he enters the confines of a tavern, claps me his sword
      upon the table and says "God send me no need of
      thee!" and by the operation of the second cup draws
8   him on the drawer, when indeed there is no need.

BENVOLIO   Am I like such a fellow?

10 MERCUTIO   Come, come, thou art as hot a Jack in thy
      mood as any in Italy; and as soon moved to be moody,
12   and as soon moody to be moved.

BENVOLIO   And what to?

_____

30–31 *Conceit . . . ornament* understanding, enriched more by the substance
than by words, takes pride in the reality of my great love, not in its outward
show   **33** *love . . . excess* (cf. II.2.135 and n.)

      III.1 A public place in Verona   **8–9** *by the operation . . . drawer* after
drinking only two cups of wine, draws his sword against the waiter   **12**
moody angry

MERCUTIO   Nay, an there were two such, we should have   15
none shortly, for one would kill the other. Thou! why,
thou wilt quarrel with a man that hath a hair more or a
hair less in his beard than thou hast. Thou wilt quarrel
with a man for cracking nuts, having no other reason
but because thou hast hazel eyes. What eye but such an   20
eye would spy out such a quarrel? Thy head is as full of   21
quarrels as an egg is full of meat; and yet thy head hath   22
been beaten as addle as an egg for quarreling. Thou   23
hast quarreled with a man for coughing in the street,
because he hath wakened thy dog that hath lain asleep
in the sun. Didst thou not fall out with a tailor for
wearing his new doublet before Easter? with another   27
for tying his new shoes with old ribbon? And yet thou
wilt tutor me from quarreling!

BENVOLIO   An I were so apt to quarrel as thou art, any   30
man should buy the fee simple of my life for an hour   31
and a quarter.

MERCUTIO   The fee simple? O simple!   33
      Enter Tybalt and others.

BENVOLIO   By my head, here come the Capulets.

MERCUTIO   By my heel, I care not.

TYBALT
Follow me close, for I will speak to them.
Gentlemen, good-den. A word with one of you.   37

MERCUTIO
And but one word with one of us?
Couple it with something; make it a word and a blow.

TYBALT   You shall find me apt enough to that, sir, an   40
you will give me occasion.

---

15 *two* (punning on Benvolio's "to")   21 *spy out* see occasion for   22 *meat* edible matter   23 *addle* addled, confused   27 *doublet* jacket   31 *fee simple* permanent lease   31–32 *hour and a quarter* probable duration of the lease – i.e., of my life   33 *O simple* O stupid; **s.d.** (Q2 includes the name "Petruccio")   37 *good-den* good afternoon

MERCUTIO   Could you not take some occasion without
    giving?

TYBALT   Mercutio, thou consortest with Romeo.

45 MERCUTIO   Consort? What, dost thou make us min-
    strels? An thou make minstrels of us, look to hear noth-
47 ing but discords. Here's my fiddlestick; here's that shall
48 make you dance. Zounds, consort!

BENVOLIO
    We talk here in the public haunt of men.
50 Either withdraw unto some private place,
    Or reason coldly of your grievances,
    Or else depart. Here all eyes gaze on us.

MERCUTIO
    Men's eyes were made to look, and let them gaze.
    I will not budge for no man's pleasure, I.
        Enter Romeo.

TYBALT
    Well, peace be with you, sir. Here comes my man.

MERCUTIO
56 But I'll be hanged, sir, if he wear your livery.
57 Marry, go before to field, he'll be your follower!
    Your worship in that sense may call him man.

TYBALT
    Romeo, the love I bear thee can afford
60 No better term than this: thou art a villain.

ROMEO
    Tybalt, the reason that I have to love thee
62 Doth much excuse the appertaining rage
    To such a greeting. Villain am I none.
    Therefore farewell. I see thou knowest me not.

---

45 *Consort* (1) associate with, (2) accompany in vocal or instrumental music;
minstrels (a more disreputable title than "musicians"; cf. IV.5.111–12)   **47**
fiddlestick i.e., rapier   **48** *Zounds* by God's wounds   **56** *livery* servant's uniform (*my man* could mean "my manservant")   **57** *field* dueling ground   **62**
appertaining rage suitably angry reaction

TYBALT
   Boy, this shall not excuse the injuries
   That thou hast done me; therefore turn and draw.
ROMEO
   I do protest I never injured thee,
   But love thee better than thou canst devise   68
   Till thou shalt know the reason of my love;
   And so, good Capulet, which name I tender   70
   As dearly as mine own, be satisfied.
MERCUTIO
   O calm, dishonorable, vile submission!
   Alla stoccata carries it away.   73
     [Draws.]
   Tybalt, you ratcatcher, will you walk?
TYBALT
   What wouldst thou have with me?
MERCUTIO   Good King of Cats, nothing but one of your
nine lives. That I mean to make bold withal, and, as 77
you shall use me hereafter, dry-beat the rest of the 78
eight. Will you pluck your sword out of his pilcher by 79
the ears? Make haste, lest mine be about your ears ere it 80
be out.
TYBALT   I am for you.
     [Draws.]
ROMEO
   Gentle Mercutio, put thy rapier up.
MERCUTIO   Come, sir, your passado!   84
     [They fight.]
ROMEO
   Draw, Benvolio; beat down their weapons.
   Gentlemen, for shame! forbear this outrage!

---

68 *devise* understand   **70** *tender* value   **73** *Alla stoccata* "at the thrust" – i.e.,
Tybalt; *carries it away* triumphs, gets away with it   **77** *nine lives* (proverbial:
a cat has nine lives); *bold withal* free with   **78** *dry-beat* thrash   **79** *pilcher*
scabbard   **84** *passado* lunge

Tybalt, Mercutio, the prince expressly hath
Forbid this bandying in Verona streets.

89   Hold, Tybalt! Good Mercutio!
        [Romeo rushes between them; Tybalt under Romeo's
        arm thrusts Mercutio in, and flies with his Followers.]
MERCUTIO   I am hurt.
90   A plague a both your houses! I am sped.
       Is he gone and hath nothing?
BENVOLIO   What, art thou hurt?
MERCUTIO
       Ay, ay, a scratch, a scratch. Marry, 'tis enough.
       Where is my page? Go, villain, fetch a surgeon.
                                              [Exit Page.]

ROMEO
       Courage, man. The hurt cannot be much.
MERCUTIO   No, 'tis not so deep as a well, nor so wide as a
       church door; but 'tis enough, 'twill serve. Ask for me
97   tomorrow, and you shall find me a grave man. I am
98   peppered, I warrant, for this world. A plague a both
       your houses! Zounds, a dog, a rat, a mouse, a cat, to
100 scratch a man to death! a braggart, a rogue, a villain,
101 that fights by the book of arithmetic! Why the devil
       came you between us? I was hurt under your arm.
ROMEO
       I thought all for the best.
MERCUTIO
       Help me into some house, Benvolio,
       Or I shall faint. A plague a both your houses!
106 They have made worms' meat of me. I have it,
       And soundly too. Your houses!
                              Exit [supported by Benvolio].

---

89 s.d. ("Tybalt . . . flies" from Q1; Q2 reads "Away Tybalt," which might be
a misplaced speech for one of Tybalt's followers – e.g., Petruccio)   **90** *a* on;
sped mortally wounded   **97** *grave* (1) serious, (2) inhabiting a grave   **98** *peppered* done for   **101** *by . . . arithmetic* by the textbook, by numbers
(cf. II.4.21)   **106** *worms' meat* i.e., a corpse; *I have it* I've bought it

ROMEO

  This gentleman, the prince's near ally,
  My very friend, hath got this mortal hurt   109
  In my behalf – my reputation stained   *110*
  With Tybalt's slander – Tybalt, that an hour
  Hath been my cousin. O sweet Juliet,
  Thy beauty hath made me effeminate
  And in my temper softened valor's steel!   114
    Enter Benvolio.

BENVOLIO

  O Romeo, Romeo, brave Mercutio is dead!
  That gallant spirit hath aspired the clouds,   116
  Which too untimely here did scorn the earth.

ROMEO

  This day's black fate on more days doth depend;   118
  This but begins the woe others must end.
    [Enter Tybalt.]

BENVOLIO

  Here comes the furious Tybalt back again.   *120*

ROMEO

  Alive in triumph, and Mercutio slain?
  Away to heaven respective lenity,   122
  And fire-eyed fury be my conduct now!   123
  Now, Tybalt, take the "villain" back again
  That late thou gavest me; for Mercutio's soul
  Is but a little way above our heads,
  Staying for thine to keep him company.
  Either thou or I, or both, must go with him.

TYBALT

  Thou, wretched boy, that didst consort him here,
  Shalt with him hence.   *130*

---

109 *very* true   **114** *temper* nature (with pun on "tempering steel")   **116** *aspired* climbed toward   **118** *depend* hang over (cf. I.4.107 and note)   **122** *respective lenity* reasoned gentleness (personified as an angel)   **123** *fire-eyed fury* (fury personified); *conduct* guide

ROMEO   This shall determine that.
    They fight. Tybalt falls.

BENVOLIO
  Romeo, away, be gone!
  The citizens are up, and Tybalt slain.
  Stand not amazed. The prince will doom thee death
  If thou art taken. Hence, be gone, away!

ROMEO
135 O, I am fortune's fool!

BENVOLIO   Why dost thou stay? *Exit Romeo.*
    Enter Citizens.

CITIZEN
  Which way ran he that killed Mercutio?
  Tybalt, that murderer, which way ran he?

BENVOLIO
  There lies that Tybalt.

CITIZEN   Up, sir, go with me.
  I charge thee in the prince's name obey.
    Enter Prince, old Montague, Capulet, their Wives,
    and all.

PRINCE
140 Where are the vile beginners of this fray?

BENVOLIO
141 O noble prince, I can discover all
142 The unlucky manage of this fatal brawl.
  There lies the man, slain by young Romeo,
  That slew thy kinsman, brave Mercutio.

CAPULET'S WIFE
  Tybalt, my cousin! O my brother's child!
  O prince! O cousin, husband! O, the blood is spilled
  Of my dear kinsman! Prince, as thou art true,
  For blood of ours shed blood of Montague.
  O cousin, cousin!

PRINCE
150 Benvolio, who began this bloody fray?

---

135 *fool* dupe, victim   **141** *discover* reveal   **142** *manage* course

BENVOLIO

    Tybalt, here slain, whom Romeo's hand did slay.

    Romeo, that spoke him fair, bid him bethink

    How nice the quarrel was, and urged withal   153

    Your high displeasure. All this – utterèd

    With gentle breath, calm look, knees humbly bowed –

    Could not take truce with the unruly spleen   156

    Of Tybalt deaf to peace, but that he tilts

    With piercing steel at bold Mercutio's breast;

    Who, all as hot, turns deadly point to point,

    And, with a martial scorn, with one hand beats   *160*

    Cold death aside and with the other sends

    It back to Tybalt, whose dexterity

    Retorts it. Romeo, he cries aloud,

    "Hold, friends! friends, part!" and swifter than his

      tongue,

    His agile arm beats down their fatal points,

    And 'twixt them rushes, underneath whose arm

    An envious thrust from Tybalt hit the life   167

    Of stout Mercutio, and then Tybalt fled.   168

    But by and by comes back to Romeo,

    Who had but newly entertained revenge,   170

    And to't they go like lightning; for, ere I

    Could draw to part them, was stout Tybalt slain;

    And, as he fell, did Romeo turn and fly.

    This is the truth, or let Benvolio die.

CAPULET'S WIFE

    He is a kinsman to the Montague;

    Affection makes him false, he speaks not true.

    Some twenty of them fought in this black strife,

    And all those twenty could but kill one life.

    I beg for justice, which thou, prince, must give.

    Romeo slew Tybalt; Romeo must not live.   *180*

---

153 *nice* trivial   156 *spleen* temper   167 *envious* malicious   168 *stout* brave
170 *entertained* harbored thoughts of

PRINCE
    Romeo slew him; he slew Mercutio.
    Who now the price of his dear blood doth owe?
MONTAGUE
    Not Romeo, prince; he was Mercutio's friend;
    His fault concludes but what the law should end,
    The life of Tybalt.
PRINCE   And for that offense
    Immediately we do exile him hence.
    I have an interest in your hate's proceeding,
    My blood for your rude brawls doth lie a-bleeding;
189   But I'll amerce you with so strong a fine
190   That you shall all repent the loss of mine.
    I will be deaf to pleading and excuses;
    Nor tears nor prayers shall purchase out abuses.
    Therefore use none. Let Romeo hence in haste,
    Else, when he is found, that hour is his last.
195   Bear hence this body, and attend our will.
    Mercy but murders, pardoning those that kill.
                                 [Exeunt.]

*

~ **III.2** *Enter Juliet alone.*

JULIET
1   Gallop apace, you fiery-footed steeds,
2   Towards Phoebus' lodging! Such a wagoner
3   As Phaeton would whip you to the west
    And bring in cloudy night immediately.
    Spread thy close curtain, love-performing night,
6   That runaways' eyes may wink, and Romeo
    Leap to these arms untalked of and unseen.

---

189 *amerce* penalize   **195** *attend our will* come to be judged
    III.2 Capulet's house   **1** *steeds* horses drawing the chariot of the sun
2 *Phoebus* the sun god; *lodging* (below the Western horizon); *wagoner* charioteer   **3** *Phaeton* Phoebus's son, who lost control of the horses and had to be killed by Jupiter   **6** *runaways' eyes* eyes of the sun's horses (?); *wink* close

Lovers can see to do their amorous rites
By their own beauties; or, if love be blind,   9
It best agrees with night. Come, civil night,   10
Thou sober-suited matron, all in black,
And learn me how to lose a winning match,
Played for a pair of stainless maidenhoods.
Hood my unmanned blood, bating in my cheeks,   14
With thy black mantle till strange love grow bold,   15
Think true love acted simple modesty.   16
Come, night; come, Romeo; come, thou day in night;
For thou wilt lie upon the wings of night
Whiter than new snow upon a raven's back.
Come, gentle night; come, loving, black-browed night;   20
Give me my Romeo; and, when I shall die,   21
Take him and cut him out in little stars,
And he will make the face of heaven so fine
That all the world will be in love with night
And pay no worship to the garish sun.
O, I have bought the mansion of a love,
But not possessed it; and though I am sold,
Not yet enjoyed. So tedious is this day
As is the night before some festival
To an impatient child that hath new robes   30
And may not wear them. O, here comes my nurse,   31
    Enter Nurse, with cords.
And she brings news; and every tongue that speaks
But Romeo's name speaks heavenly eloquence.
Now, nurse, what news? What hast thou there, the cords
That Romeo bid thee fetch?
NURSE   Ay, ay, the cords.
    [Throws them down.]

---

9 *love* Cupid   14 *Hood* cover with a hood; *unmanned* untamed, unmarried;
bating fluttering (all three are terms in falconry)   15 *strange* reserved, diffi-
dent   16 *true love acted* the act of true love   21 *I* (often emended to "he,"
following Q4, but Juliet may be more selfish than that; she may also be punning on "die" as "orgasm")   31 **s.d.** *cords* rope ladder (In Q1 the s.d. reads
"Enter the Nurse, wringing her hands, with the ladder of cords in her lap.")

JULIET

    Ay me! what news? Why dost thou wring thy hands?

NURSE

37   Ah, welladay! he's dead, he's dead, he's dead!

    We are undone, lady, we are undone!

    Alack the day! he's gone, he's killed, he's dead!

JULIET

40   Can heaven be so envious?

NURSE   Romeo can,

    Though heaven cannot. O Romeo, Romeo!

    Who ever would have thought it? Romeo!

JULIET

    What devil art thou that dost torment me thus?

    This torture should be roared in dismal hell.

45   Hath Romeo slain himself? Say thou but "Ay,"

    And that bare vowel "I" shall poison more

47   Than the death-darting eye of cockatrice.

    I am not I, if there be such an "Ay"

    Or those eyes shut that makes thee answer "Ay."

50   If he be slain, say "Ay"; or if not, "No."

    Brief sounds determine of my weal or woe.

NURSE

    I saw the wound, I saw it with mine eyes

53   (God save the mark!), here on his manly breast.

    A piteous corpse, a bloody piteous corpse,

    Pale, pale as ashes, all bedaubed in blood,

56   All in gore blood. I swoonèd at the sight.

JULIET

    O, break, my heart! poor bankrupt, break at once!

    To prison, eyes; ne'er look on liberty!

59   Vile earth, to earth resign; end motion here,

60   And thou and Romeo press one heavy bier!

---

37 *welladay* alas 40 *envious* malicious 45–50 *I, Ay* (there is a sustained pun on the homophones "I" and "Ay") 47 *cockatrice* basilisk (a fabulous serpent that killed with eye glances) 53 *God . . . mark* God avert the evil omen 56 *gore blood* clotted blood 59 *Vile earth* i.e., my body; *resign* return

NURSE
    O Tybalt, Tybalt, the best friend I had!
    O courteous Tybalt! honest gentleman!
    That ever I should live to see thee dead!
JULIET
    What storm is this that blows so contrary?
    Is Romeo slaughtered, and is Tybalt dead?
    My dearest cousin, and my dearer lord?
    Then, dreadful trumpet, sound the general doom!   67
    For who is living, if those two are gone?
NURSE
    Tybalt is gone, and Romeo banishèd;
    Romeo that killed him, he is banishèd.   70
JULIET
    O God! Did Romeo's hand shed Tybalt's blood?
NURSE
    It did, it did! alas the day, it did!   72
JULIET
    O serpent heart, hid with a flow'ring face!   73
    Did ever dragon keep so fair a cave?
    Beautiful tyrant! fiend angelical!   75
    Dove-feathered raven! wolvish-ravening lamb!   76
    Despisèd substance of divinest show!
    Just opposite to what thou justly seem'st –
    A damnèd saint, an honorable villain!
    O nature, what hadst thou to do in hell   80
    When thou didst bower the spirit of a fiend   81
    In mortal paradise of such sweet flesh?
    Was ever book containing such vile matter
    So fairly bound? O, that deceit should dwell
    In such a gorgeous palace!

---

67 *trumpet* i.e., the "last trumpet"; *general doom* Judgment Day   **72, 73** (in
Q2 l. 72 is mistakenly assigned to Juliet, l. 73 to the nurse)   **73** *flow'ring
face* (traditionally, the Serpent in Eden appeared to Eve with the face of a
young girl, wreathed in flowers)   **75** *fiend angelical* (cf. 2 Corinthians 11:14)
76 *wolvish-ravening lamb* (cf. Matthew 7:15)   **81–82** *bower* lodge; *spirit . . .
paradise* i.e., the Serpent in Eden

NURSE   There's no trust,
   No faith, no honesty in men; all perjured,
   All forsworn, all naught, all dissemblers.
88   Ah, where's my man? Give me some aqua vitae.
   These griefs, these woes, these sorrows make me old.
90   Shame come to Romeo!
JULIET   Blistered be thy tongue
   For such a wish! He was not born to shame.
   Upon his brow shame is ashamed to sit,
   For 'tis a throne where honor may be crowned
   Sole monarch of the universal earth.
   O, what a beast was I to chide at him!
NURSE
   Will you speak well of him that killed your cousin?
JULIET
   Shall I speak ill of him that is my husband?
   Ah, poor my lord, what tongue shall smooth thy name
   When I, thy three-hours wife, have mangled it?
100   But wherefore, villain, didst thou kill my cousin?
   That villain cousin would have killed my husband.
   Back, foolish tears, back to your native spring!
103   Your tributary drops belong to woe,
   Which you, mistaking, offer up to joy.
   My husband lives, that Tybalt would have slain;
   And Tybalt's dead, that would have slain my husband.
   All this is comfort; wherefore weep I then?
   Some word there was, worser than Tybalt's death,
   That murdered me. I would forget it fain;
110   But O, it presses to my memory
   Like damnèd guilty deeds to sinners' minds!
   "Tybalt is dead, and Romeo – banishèd."
   That "banishèd," that one word "banishèd,"
   Hath slain ten thousand Tybalts. Tybalt's death
   Was woe enough, if it had ended there;

---

88 *aqua vitae* alcoholic spirits   103 *tributary* tribute-paying

Or, if sour woe delights in fellowship
And needly will be ranked with other griefs,   117
Why followed not, when she said "Tybalt's dead,"
Thy father, or thy mother, nay, or both,
Which modern lamentation might have moved?   120
But with a rearward following Tybalt's death,   121
"Romeo is banishèd" – to speak that word
Is father, mother, Tybalt, Romeo, Juliet,
All slain, all dead. "Romeo is banishèd" –
There is no end, no limit, measure, bound,
In that word's death; no words can that woe sound.
Where is my father and my mother, nurse?

NURSE

Weeping and wailing over Tybalt's corpse.   128
Will you go to them? I will bring you thither.

JULIET

Wash they his wounds with tears? Mine shall be spent,   130
When theirs are dry, for Romeo's banishment.
Take up those cords. Poor ropes, you are beguiled,
Both you and I, for Romeo is exiled.
He made you for a highway to my bed;
But I, a maid, die maiden-widowèd.
Come, cords; come, nurse. I'll to my wedding bed;
And death, not Romeo, take my maidenhead!

NURSE

Hie to your chamber. I'll find Romeo
To comfort you. I wot well where he is.   139
Hark ye, your Romeo will be here at night.   140
I'll to him; he is hid at Laurence' cell.

JULIET

O, find him! give this ring to my true knight
And bid him come to take his last farewell.
                                        Exit [with Nurse].

                              ✱

117 *needly* necessarily 120 *modern* ordinary, conventional 121 *rearward*
rear guard 128 *corpse* body 139 *wot* know

∾ **III.3** *Enter Friar [Laurence].*

FRIAR
1   Romeo, come forth; come forth, thou fearful man.
2   Affliction is enamored of thy parts,
     And thou art wedded to calamity.
          Enter Romeo.
ROMEO
4   Father, what news? What is the prince's doom?
     What sorrow craves acquaintance at my hand
     That I yet know not?
FRIAR   Too familiar
     Is my dear son with such sour company.
     I bring thee tidings of the prince's doom.
ROMEO
9   What less than doomsday is the prince's doom?
FRIAR
10   A gentler judgment vanished from his lips –
     Not body's death, but body's banishment.
ROMEO
     Ha, banishment? Be merciful, say "death";
     For exile hath more terror in his look,
     Much more than death. Do not say "banishment."
FRIAR
     Hence from Verona art thou banishèd.
     Be patient, for the world is broad and wide.
ROMEO
     There is no world without Verona walls,
     But purgatory, torture, hell itself.
     Hence banishèd is banished from the world,

III.3 Friar Laurence's cell **s.d.** (Separate entrances in Q1; Q2 reads "Enter Friar and Romeo.") **1** *fearful* full of fear **2** *parts* qualities **4** *prince's doom* punishment decreed by the prince **9** *doomsday* i.e., death **10** *vanished* disappeared into air

And world's exile is death. Then "banishèd"   20
Is death mistermed. Calling death "banishèd,"
Thou cut'st my head off with a golden ax
And smilest upon the stroke that murders me.

FRIAR
O deadly sin! O rude unthankfulness!
Thy fault our law calls death; but the kind prince,
Taking thy part, hath rushed aside the law,   26
And turned that black word "death" to banishment.
This is dear mercy, and thou seest it not.

ROMEO
'Tis torture, and not mercy. Heaven is here,
Where Juliet lives; and every cat and dog   30
And little mouse, every unworthy thing,
Live here in heaven and may look on her;
But Romeo may not. More validity,   33
More honorable state, more courtship lives   34
In carrion flies than Romeo. They may seize
On the white wonder of dear Juliet's hand
And steal immortal blessing from her lips,
Who, even in pure and vestal modesty,   38
Still blush, as thinking their own kisses sin;   39
But Romeo may not, he is banishèd.   40
Flies may do this but I from this must fly;
They are free men, but I am banishèd.
And sayest thou yet that exile is not death?
Hadst thou no poison mixed, no sharp-ground knife,
No sudden mean of death, though ne'er so mean,   45
But "banishèd" to kill me – "banishèd"?
O friar, the damnèd use that word in hell;
Howling attends it! How hast thou the heart,
Being a divine, a ghostly confessor,

---

26 *rushed* pushed   33 *validity* value   34 *courtship* privilege of wooing   38
vestal virgin   39 *kisses* (when her lips touch each other)   40–42 (in Q2 these
lines are preceded by "This may flies do when I from this must fly" – evidently a canceled line printed in error – and by l. 43, evidently misplaced)
45 *mean . . . mean* means . . . lowly

50 A sin absolver, and my friend professed,
   To mangle me with that word "banishèd"?

FRIAR

52 Thou fond mad man, hear me a little speak.

ROMEO

O, thou wilt speak again of banishment.

FRIAR

I'll give thee armor to keep off that word;
Adversity's sweet milk, philosophy,
To comfort thee, though thou art banishèd.

ROMEO

Yet "banishèd"? Hang up philosophy!
Unless philosophy can make a Juliet,
Displant a town, reverse a prince's doom,
60 It helps not, it prevails not. Talk no more.

FRIAR

O, then I see that madmen have no ears.

ROMEO

How should they, when that wise men have no eyes?

FRIAR

63 Let me dispute with thee of thy estate.

ROMEO

Thou canst not speak of that thou dost not feel.
Wert thou as young as I, Juliet thy love,
An hour but married, Tybalt murderèd,
Doting like me, and like me banishèd,
Then mightst thou speak, then mightst thou tear thy
   hair,
And fall upon the ground, as I do now,
70 Taking the measure of an unmade grave.
   Knock [within].

FRIAR

Arise; one knocks. Good Romeo, hide thyself.

---

52 *fond* foolish   **63** *dispute* reason; *estate* situation   **70** *Taking the measure*
providing the measurements; **s.d.** (Q2 reads "Enter Nurse and knock," giving her another entrance after l. 78)

ROMEO
  Not I, unless the breath of heartsick groans
  Mistlike enfold me from the search of eyes.   73
    [Knock.]
FRIAR
  Hark, how they knock! Who's there? Romeo, arise;
  Thou wilt be taken. – Stay awhile! – Stand up;   75
    [Knock.]
  Run to my study. – By and by! – God's will,   76
  What simpleness is this. – I come, I come!   77
    Knock.
  Who knocks so hard? Whence come you? What's your
    will?
    Enter Nurse.
NURSE
  Let me come in, and you shall know my errand.
  I come from Lady Juliet.   *80*
FRIAR   Welcome then.
NURSE
  O holy friar, O, tell me, holy friar,
  Where is my lady's lord, where's Romeo?
FRIAR
  There on the ground, with his own tears made drunk.
NURSE
  O, he is even in my mistress' case,
  Just in her case! O woeful sympathy!
  Piteous predicament! Even so lies she,
  Blubb'ring and weeping, weeping and blubb'ring.
  Stand up, stand up! Stand, an you be a man.
  For Juliet's sake, for her sake, rise and stand!
  Why should you fall into so deep an O?   90
ROMEO   *[Rises.]* Nurse –

---

73 **s.d.** (Q2 reads "They knock.")   75 **s.d.** (Q2 reads "Slud knock.")   76 *By and by* in a moment   77 *simpleness* stupid conduct   **90** *an O* a fit of groaning (throughout this speech, the nurse's language is full of unintentional sexual puns on "case," "stand," rise," "O")

NURSE
    Ah sir! ah sir! Death's the end of all.

ROMEO
    Speakest thou of Juliet? How is it with her?
94 Doth not she think me an old murderer,
    Now I have stained the childhood of our joy
    With blood removed but little from her own?
    Where is she? and how doth she? and what says
98 My concealed lady to our canceled love?

NURSE
    O, she says nothing, sir, but weeps and weeps;
100 And now falls on her bed, and then starts up,
    And Tybalt calls; and then on Romeo cries,
    And then down falls again.

ROMEO   As if that name,
103 Shot from the deadly level of a gun,
    Did murder her; as that name's cursèd hand
    Murdered her kinsman. O, tell me, friar, tell me,
106 In what vile part of this anatomy
    Doth my name lodge? Tell me, that I may sack
108 The hateful mansion.
        [He offers to stab himself, and Nurse snatches the
        dagger away.]

FRIAR   Hold thy desperate hand.
    Art thou a man? Thy form cries out thou art;
110 Thy tears are womanish, thy wild acts denote
111 The unreasonable fury of a beast.
112 Unseemly woman in a seeming man!
113 And ill-beseeming beast in seeming both!
    Thou hast amazed me. By my holy order,
    I thought thy disposition better tempered.
    Hast thou slain Tybalt? Wilt thou slay thyself?

---

94 *old* hardened 98 *concealed . . . canceled* secret (wife) . . . invalidated by my act (the two words were given almost the same pronunciation) 103 *level* aim 106 *anatomy* body 108 s.d. (from Q1) 111 *unreasonable* irrational 112 *Unseemly . . . seeming* disorderly . . . apparent 113 *ill-beseeming . . . both* inappropriate . . . man and woman

And slay thy lady that in thy life lives,   117
By doing damnèd hate upon thyself?
Why railest thou on thy birth, the heaven, and earth?
Since birth and heaven and earth, all three do meet   120
In thee at once, which thou at once wouldst lose.
Fie, fie, thou shamest thy shape, thy love, thy wit,
Which, like a usurer, abound'st in all,   123
And usest none in that true use indeed   124
Which should bedeck thy shape, thy love, thy wit.
Thy noble shape is but a form of wax,   126
Digressing from the valor of a man;
Thy dear love sworn but hollow perjury,
Killing that love which thou hast vowed to cherish;   129
Thy wit, that ornament to shape and love,   130
Misshapen in the conduct of them both,   131
Like powder in a skill-less soldier's flask,   132
Is set afire by thine own ignorance,
And thou dismembered with thine own defense.   134
What, rouse thee, man! Thy Juliet is alive,
For whose dear sake thou wast but lately dead.   136
There art thou happy. Tybalt would kill thee,   137
But thou slewest Tybalt. There art thou happy too.
The law, that threatened death, becomes thy friend
And turns it to exile. There art thou happy.   *140*
A pack of blessings light upon thy back;
Happiness courts thee in her best array;
But, like a mishavèd and sullen wench,   143
Thou pout'st upon thy fortune and thy love.
Take heed, take heed, for such die miserable.
Go get thee to thy love, as was decreed,

---

117 *in . . . lives* (cf. II.1.1 and n.)   120 *all . . . meet* the soul comes from
heaven, the body from earth; they unite in man at his birth   123 *Which*
(you) who; *all* all capabilities   124 *true use* proper purpose   126 *form of
wax* waxwork, outward appearance   129 *Killing that love* (cf. l. 117)   130
wit intellect   131 *Misshapen* distorted; *conduct* guidance   132 *flask* powder
horn   134 *defense* i.e., intellect   136 *dead* as one dead   137 *happy* fortu-
nate   143 *mishavèd* misbehaved

Ascend her chamber, hence and comfort her.
But look thou stay not till the watch be set,
For then thou canst not pass to Mantua,
150 Where thou shalt live till we can find a time
151 To blaze your marriage, reconcile your friends,
Beg pardon of the prince, and call thee back
With twenty hundred thousand times more joy
Than thou went'st forth in lamentation.
Go before, nurse. Commend me to thy lady,
And bid her hasten all the house to bed,
Which heavy sorrow makes them apt unto.
Romeo is coming.

NURSE
O Lord, I could have stayed here all the night
160 To hear good counsel. O, what learning is!
My lord, I'll tell my lady you will come.

ROMEO
162 Do so, and bid my sweet prepare to chide.
   [Nurse offers to go in, and turns again.]

NURSE
Here, sir, a ring she bid me give you, sir.
Hie you, make haste, for it grows very late.

ROMEO
How well my comfort is revived by this!
                                    [Exit Nurse.]

FRIAR
166 Go hence; good night; and here stands all your state:
Either be gone before the watch be set,
Or by the break of day disguised from hence.
Sojourn in Mantua. I'll find out your man,
170 And he shall signify from time to time
Every good hap to you that chances here.
Give me thy hand. 'Tis late. Farewell, good night.

---

151 *blaze* publish   **162 s.d.** (from Q1)   **166** *here . . . state* here is your
whole situation

ROMEO
    But that a joy past joy calls out on me,
    It were a grief so brief to part with thee.   174
    Farewell.   *Exeunt.*

*

❧ **III.4** *Enter old Capulet, his Wife, and Paris.*

CAPULET
    Things have fall'n out, sir, so unluckily
    That we have had no time to move our daughter.   2
    Look you, she loved her kinsman Tybalt dearly,
    And so did I. Well, we were born to die.
    'Tis very late; she'll not come down tonight.
    I promise you, but for your company,
    I would have been abed an hour ago.
PARIS
    These times of woe afford no times to woo.
    Madam, good night. Commend me to your daughter.
CAPULET'S WIFE
    I will, and know her mind early tomorrow;   *10*
    Tonight she's mewed up to her heaviness.   11
        [Paris offers to go in, and Capulet calls him again.]
CAPULET
    Sir Paris, I will make a desperate tender   12
    Of my child's love. I think she will be ruled
    In all respects by me; nay more, I doubt it not.
    Wife, go you to her ere you go to bed;
    Acquaint her here of my son Paris' love
    And bid her (mark you me?) on Wednesday next –
    But soft! what day is this?
PARIS   Monday, my lord.

---

174 *brief* hastily
    III.4 Capulet's house **2** *move* persuade **11** *mewed up* shut up (fal-
conry); *heaviness* grief; **s.d.** (from Q1) **12** *desperate tender* risk-taking offer

CAPULET
  Monday! ha, ha! Well, Wednesday is too soon.
20 A Thursday let it be – a Thursday, tell her,
  She shall be married to this noble earl.
  Will you be ready? Do you like this haste?
  We'll keep no great ado – a friend or two;
  For hark you, Tybalt being slain so late,
  It may be thought we held him carelessly,
  Being our kinsman, if we revel much.
  Therefore we'll have some half a dozen friends,
  And there an end. But what say you to Thursday?
PARIS
  My lord, I would that Thursday were tomorrow.
CAPULET
30 Well, get you gone. A Thursday be it then.
  Go you to Juliet ere you go to bed;
  Prepare her, wife, against this wedding day.
  Farewell, my lord. – Light to my chamber, ho!
34 Afore me, it is so very very late
35 That we may call it early by and by.
  Good night.   *Exeunt.*

                        ✳

  ∾ **III.5** *Enter Romeo and Juliet aloft [at the window].*

JULIET
  Wilt thou be gone? It is not yet near day.
  It was the nightingale, and not the lark,
3 That pierced the fearful hollow of thine ear.
  Nightly she sings on yond pomegranate tree.
  Believe me, love, it was the nightingale.
ROMEO
  It was the lark, the herald of the morn;
  No nightingale. Look, love, what envious streaks

---

20 *A* on   **34** *Afore me* (a light oath)   **35** *by and by* immediately
  III.5 s.d. *at the window* (from Q1)   **3** *fearful* apprehensive

Do lace the severing clouds in yonder east.
Night's candles are burnt out, and jocund day   9
Stands tiptoe on the misty mountaintops.   10
I must be gone and live, or stay and die.

JULIET
Yond light is not daylight; I know it, I.
It is some meteor that the sun exhales   13
To be to thee this night a torchbearer
And light thee on thy way to Mantua.
Therefore stay yet; thou need'st not to be gone.

ROMEO
Let me be ta'en, let me be put to death.
I am content, so thou wilt have it so.
I'll say yon gray is not the morning's eye,
'Tis but the pale reflex of Cynthia's brow;   20
Nor that is not the lark whose notes do beat
The vaulty heaven so high above our heads.
I have more care to stay than will to go.
Come, death, and welcome! Juliet wills it so.
How is't, my soul? Let's talk; it is not day.   25

JULIET
It is, it is! Hie hence, be gone, away!
It is the lark that sings so out of tune,
Straining harsh discords and unpleasing sharps.
Some say the lark makes sweet division;   29
This doth not so, for she divideth us.   30
Some say the lark and loathèd toad change eyes;   31
O, now I would they had changed voices too,
Since arm from arm that voice doth us affray,   33
Hunting thee hence with hunt's-up to the day.   34
O, now be gone! More light and light it grows.

---

9 *Night's candles* the stars   **13** *meteor* nocturnal light, such as the will-o'-the-wisp, supposedly of luminous gas given off by the sun or drawn by his power (*exhales*) out of marshy ground   **20** *reflex . . . brow* reflection of the moon   **25** *my soul* (cf. II.2.165)   **29** *division* ornaments on a melody   **31** *change* exchange (a folk belief)   **33** *affray* frighten   **34** *hunt's-up* morning song to awaken huntsmen

ROMEO

36   More light and light – more dark and dark our woes.
         Enter Nurse [hastily].

NURSE   Madam!

JULIET   Nurse?

NURSE

      Your lady mother is coming to your chamber.

40   The day is broke; be wary, look about.   *[Exit.]*

JULIET

41   Then, window, let day in, and let life out.

ROMEO

42   Farewell, farewell! One kiss, and I'll descend.
         [He goeth down.]

JULIET

43   Art thou gone so, love, lord, my husband, friend?
      I must hear from thee every day in the hour,
      For in a minute there are many days.

46   O, by this count I shall be much in years
      Ere I again behold my Romeo!

ROMEO

      Farewell!
      I will omit no opportunity

50   That may convey my greetings, love, to thee.

JULIET

      O, think'st thou we shall ever meet again?

ROMEO

      I doubt it not; and all these woes shall serve
      For sweet discourses in our times to come.

JULIET

54   O God, I have an ill-divining soul!
      Methinks I see thee, now thou art so low,
      As one dead in the bottom of a tomb.
      Either my eyesight fails, or thou lookest pale.

------

36 s.d. *hastily* (From Q1; Q2 reads "Enter Madam and Nurse.") **41** *life* (cf. III.3.117) **42 s.d.** (from Q1) **43** *friend* lover **46** *much* advanced **54** *ill-divining* prophetic of evil

ROMEO
    And trust me, love, in my eye so do you.
    Dry sorrow drinks our blood. Adieu, adieu!   *Exit.* 59
JULIET
    O Fortune, Fortune! all men call thee fickle.   60
    If thou art fickle, what dost thou with him
    That is renowned for faith? Be fickle, Fortune,
    For then I hope thou wilt not keep him long
    But send him back.   64
      [She goeth down from the window.]
      Enter [Capulet's Wife].
CAPULET'S WIFE
    Ho, daughter! are you up?
JULIET
    Who is't that calls? It is my lady mother.
    Is she not down so late, or up so early?   67
    What unaccustomed cause procures her hither?
CAPULET'S WIFE
    Why, how now, Juliet?
JULIET   Madam, I am not well.
CAPULET'S WIFE
    Evermore weeping for your cousin's death?   70
    What, wilt thou wash him from his grave with tears?
    An if thou couldst, thou couldst not make him live.
    Therefore have done. Some grief shows much of love;
    But much of grief shows still some want of wit.
JULIET
    Yet let me weep for such a feeling loss.   75
CAPULET'S WIFE
    So shall you feel the loss, but not the friend
    Which you weep for.

---

59 *Dry . . . blood* (the presumed effect of grief was to dry up the blood) **64 s.d.** (from Q1, and so placed that it might apply only to the nurse; but since the Q1 stage direction immediately following is "Enter Juliet's Mother, Nurse," the indications are that the subsequent action takes place below, where Juliet joins her mother; hence the orchard into which Romeo has descended now becomes an interior) **67** *down* abed **75** *feeling* deeply felt

JULIET   Feeling so the loss,
   I cannot choose but ever weep the friend.
CAPULET'S WIFE
   Well, girl, thou weep'st not so much for his death
80   As that the villain lives which slaughtered him.
JULIET
   What villain, madam?
CAPULET'S WIFE   That same villain Romeo.
JULIET   *[Aside]*
   Villain and he be many miles asunder. –
   God pardon him! I do, with all my heart;
84   And yet no man like he doth grieve my heart.
CAPULET'S WIFE
   That is because the traitor murderer lives.
JULIET
   Ay, madam, from the reach of these my hands.
   Would none but I might venge my cousin's death!
CAPULET'S WIFE
   We will have vengeance for it, fear thou not.
   Then weep no more. I'll send to one in Mantua,
90   Where that same banished runagate doth live,
   Shall give him such an unaccustomed dram
   That he shall soon keep Tybalt company;
   And then I hope thou wilt be satisfied.
JULIET
   Indeed I never shall be satisfied
   With Romeo till I behold him – dead –
   Is my poor heart so for a kinsman vexed.
   Madam, if you could find out but a man
98   To bear a poison, I would temper it,
   That Romeo should, upon receipt thereof,
100   Soon sleep in quiet. O, how my heart abhors
   To hear him named and cannot come to him,

---

84 *like* so much as   90 *runagate* renegade   98 *temper* prepare or concoct
(with play on "moderate")

To wreak the love I bore my cousin
Upon his body that hath slaughtered him!

CAPULET'S WIFE
Find thou the means, and I'll find such a man.
But now I'll tell thee joyful tidings, girl.

JULIET
And joy comes well in such a needy time.
What are they, beseech your ladyship?

CAPULET'S WIFE
Well, well, thou hast a careful father, child;
One who, to put thee from thy heaviness,
Hath sorted out a sudden day of joy   110
That thou expects not nor I looked not for.

JULIET
Madam, in happy time! What day is that?   112

CAPULET'S WIFE
Marry, my child, early next Thursday morn
The gallant, young, and noble gentleman,
The County Paris, at Saint Peter's Church,
Shall happily make thee there a joyful bride.

JULIET
Now by Saint Peter's Church, and Peter too,
He shall not make me there a joyful bride!
I wonder at this haste, that I must wed
Ere he that should be husband comes to woo.   120
I pray you tell my lord and father, madam,
I will not marry yet; and when I do, I swear
It shall be Romeo, whom you know I hate,
Rather than Paris. These are news indeed!

CAPULET'S WIFE
Here comes your father. Tell him so yourself,
And see how he will take it at your hands.
    Enter Capulet and Nurse.

CAPULET
When the sun sets, the earth doth drizzle dew,

---

110 *sorted* chosen **112** *in happy time* opportunely

But for the sunset of my brother's son
It rains downright.
130　How now? a conduit, girl? What, still in tears?
Evermore show'ring! In one little body
Thou counterfeit'st a bark, a sea, a wind:
For still thy eyes, which I may call the sea,
Do ebb and flow with tears; the bark thy body is,
Sailing in this salt flood; the winds, thy sighs,
Who, raging with thy tears and they with them,
137　Without a sudden calm will overset
Thy tempest-tossèd body. How now, wife?
Have you delivered to her our decree?

CAPULET'S WIFE

140　Ay, sir; but she will none, she gives you thanks.
141　I would the fool were married to her grave!

CAPULET

142　Soft! take me with you, take me with you, wife.
How? Will she none? Doth she not give us thanks?
Is she not proud? Doth she not count her blest,
145　Unworthy as she is, that we have wrought
146　So worthy a gentleman to be her bride?

JULIET

Not proud you have, but thankful that you have.
Proud can I never be of what I hate,
But thankful even for hate that is meant love.

CAPULET

150　How, how, how, how, chopped logic? What is this?
"Proud" – and "I thank you" – and "I thank you not" –
152　And yet "not proud"? Mistress minion you,
Thank me no thankings, nor proud me no prouds,
154　But fettle your fine joints 'gainst Thursday next

---

130 *conduit* water pipe　137 *sudden* immediate　140 *gives you thanks* says
"No, thank you"　141 *married . . . grave* (a petulant but prophetic comment, like l. 167 below)　142 *take . . . you* let me understand you　145
wrought arranged for　146 *bride* bridegroom　150 *chopped logic* hair-
splitting　152 *minion* spoiled child　154 *fettle* prepare

To go with Paris to Saint Peter's Church,
Or I will drag thee on a hurdle thither.   156
Out, you greensickness carrion! out, you baggage!   157
You tallow-face!   158
CAPULET'S WIFE   Fie, fie! what, are you mad?
JULIET   *[Kneeling]*
Good father, I beseech you on my knees,
Hear me with patience but to speak a word.   160
CAPULET
Hang thee, young baggage! disobedient wretch!
I tell thee what – get thee to church a Thursday   162
Or never after look me in the face.
Speak not, reply not, do not answer me!
My fingers itch. Wife, we scarce thought us blest
That God had lent us but this only child;
But now I see this one is one too much,
And that we have a curse in having her.
Out on her, hilding!   169
NURSE   God in heaven bless her!
You are to blame, my lord, to rate her so.   170
CAPULET
And why, my Lady Wisdom? Hold your tongue,
Good Prudence. Smatter with your gossips, go!   172
NURSE
I speak no treason.   173
CAPULET   O, God-i-god-en!
NURSE
May not one speak?
CAPULET   Peace, you mumbling fool!
Utter your gravity o'er a gossip's bowl,
For here we need it not.

---

156 *hurdle* sledge on which criminals were carried to execution   157 *green-sickness* anemic; *baggage* worthless woman   158 *tallow-face* pale-face; *are you mad* (addressed to Capulet)   162 *a* on   169 *hilding* worthless creature   170 *rate* scold   172 *Smatter . . . gossips* chatter with your cronies   173 *God-i-god-en* for God's sake

CAPULET'S WIFE   You are too hot.
CAPULET
177   God's bread! it makes me mad.
178   Day, night, hour, tide, time, work, play,
       Alone, in company; still my care hath been
180   To have her matched; and having now provided
       A gentleman of noble parentage,
182   Of fair demesnes, youthful, and nobly lined,
       Stuffed, as they say, with honorable parts,
       Proportioned as one's thought would wish a man –
185   And then to have a wretched puling fool,
186   A whining mammet, in her fortune's tender,
       To answer "I'll not wed, I cannot love;
       I am too young, I pray you pardon me"!
189   But, an you will not wed, I'll pardon you!
190   Graze where you will, you shall not house with me.
191   Look to't, think on't; I do not use to jest.
192   Thursday is near; lay hand on heart, advise:
       An you be mine, I'll give you to my friend;
       An you be not, hang, beg, starve, die in the streets,
       For, by my soul, I'll ne'er acknowledge thee,
       Nor what is mine shall never do thee good.
       Trust to't. Bethink you. I'll not be forsworn.   *Exit.*
JULIET
       Is there no pity sitting in the clouds
       That sees into the bottom of my grief?
200   O sweet my mother, cast me not away!
       Delay this marriage for a month, a week,

---

176 *hot* impatient   **177** *bread* bread of the sacrament of communion   **178–79** *Day . . . company* (In Q1 the equivalent passage occupies two separate lines: "Day, night, early, late, at home, abroad, / Alone, in company, waking or sleeping" – which is more logical. Q2's "hour, tide, time" might be part of an early draft.)   **182** *demesnes* domains; *lined* descended, endowed with qualities (Q1 reads "trained")   **185** *puling* whining   **186** *mammet* doll; *tender* offer   **189** *I'll pardon you* (ironic)   **191** *do not use* am not accustomed   **192** *advise* consider

Or if you do not, make the bridal bed
In that dim monument where Tybalt lies.
CAPULET'S WIFE
  Talk not to me, for I'll not speak a word.
  Do as thou wilt, for I have done with thee.   *Exit.*
JULIET
  O God! – O nurse, how shall this be prevented?
  My husband is on earth, my faith in heaven.   207
  How shall that faith return again to earth   208
  Unless that husband send it me from heaven
  By leaving earth? Comfort me, counsel me.   *210*
  Alack, alack, that heaven should practice stratagems
  Upon so soft a subject as myself!
  What say'st thou? Hast thou not a word of joy?
  Some comfort, nurse.
NURSE   Faith, here it is.
  Romeo is banished; and all the world to nothing   215
  That he dares ne'er come back to challenge you;   216
  Or if he do, it needs must be by stealth.
  Then, since the case so stands as now it doth,
  I think it best you married with the county.
  O, he's a lovely gentleman!   *220*
  Romeo's a dishclout to him. An eagle, madam,   221
  Hath not so green, so quick, so fair an eye
  As Paris hath. Beshrew my very heart,
  I think you are happy in this second match,
  For it excels your first; or if it did not,
  Your first is dead – or 'twere as good he were
  As living here and you no use of him.   227
JULIET
  Speak'st thou from thy heart?

---

207 *my faith in heaven* my marriage vow is recorded in heaven **208–10** *How . . . earth* how can I marry unless I am first widowed **215** *all . . . nothing* i.e., it is a safe bet **216** *challenge* demand possession of **221** *dishclout* dishcloth **227** *here* i.e., on earth

NURSE

229   And from my soul too; else beshrew them both.

230   JULIET   Amen!

NURSE   What?

JULIET

Well, thou hast comforted me marvelous much.

Go in and tell my lady I am gone,

Having displeased my father, to Laurence' cell,

To make confession and to be absolved.

NURSE

236   Marry, I will, and this is wisely done.   *[Exit.]*

JULIET   *[She looks after Nurse.]*

237   Ancient damnation! O most wicked fiend!

Is it more sin to wish me thus forsworn,

Or to dispraise my lord with that same tongue

240   Which she hath praised him with above compare

So many thousand times? Go, counselor!

242   Thou and my bosom henceforth shall be twain.

I'll to the friar to know his remedy.

If all else fail, myself have power to die.   *Exit.*

✳

❧ **IV.1** *Enter Friar [Laurence] and County Paris.*

FRIAR

On Thursday, sir? The time is very short.

PARIS

My father Capulet will have it so,

And I am nothing slow to slack his haste.

FRIAR

You say you do not know the lady's mind.

Uneven is the course; I like it not.

---

229 *beshrew* a curse on **236 s.d.** (from Q1) **237** *Ancient damnation* damnable old woman **242** *bosom* confidence; *twain* separated

   IV.1 Friar Laurence's cell

PARIS
>   Immoderately she weeps for Tybalt's death,
>   And therefore have I little talk of love;
>   For Venus smiles not in a house of tears.   8
>   Now, sir, her father counts it dangerous
>   That she do give her sorrow so much sway,   10
>   And in his wisdom hastes our marriage
>   To stop the inundation of her tears,
>   Which, too much minded by herself alone,   13
>   May be put from her by society.
>   Now do you know the reason of this haste.

FRIAR   *[Aside]*
>   I would I knew not why it should be slowed. –
>   Look, sir, here comes the lady toward my cell.
>   *Enter Juliet.*

PARIS
>   Happily met, my lady and my wife!

JULIET
>   That may be, sir, when I may be a wife.

PARIS
>   That "may be" must be, love, on Thursday next.   20

JULIET
>   What must be shall be.

FRIAR   That's a certain text.

PARIS
>   Come you to make confession to this father?

JULIET
>   To answer that, I should confess to you.

PARIS
>   Do not deny to him that you love me.

JULIET
>   I will confess to you that I love him.

---

8 *Venus . . . tears* the influence of the planet Venus is unfavorable when she
appears in the "house" of a "moist" constellation, such as Pisces or Aquarius;
i.e., one cannot talk of love amidst grief   13 *minded* thought about

PARIS
   So will ye, I am sure, that you love me.
JULIET
   If I do so, it will be of more price,
   Being spoke behind your back, than to your face.
PARIS
   Poor soul, thy face is much abused with tears.
JULIET
30   The tears have got small victory by that,
   For it was bad enough before their spite.
PARIS
   Thou wrong'st it more than tears with that report.
JULIET
   That is no slander, sir, which is a truth;
   And what I spake, I spake it to my face.
PARIS
   Thy face is mine, and thou hast slandered it.
JULIET
   It may be so, for it is not mine own.
   Are you at leisure, holy father, now,
   Or shall I come to you at evening Mass?
FRIAR
   My leisure serves me, pensive daughter, now.
40   My lord, we must entreat the time alone.
PARIS
41   God shield I should disturb devotion!
   Juliet, on Thursday early will I rouse ye.
   Till then, adieu, and keep this holy kiss.   *Exit.*
JULIET
   O, shut the door! and when thou hast done so,
   Come weep with me – past hope, past cure, past help!
FRIAR
   O, Juliet, I already know thy grief;
47   It strains me past the compass of my wits.

---

41 *shield* forbid   **47** *the compass . . . wits* my wit's end

I hear thou must, and nothing may prorogue it, 48
On Thursday next be married to this county.

JULIET

Tell me not, friar, that thou hearest of this, 50
Unless thou tell me how I may prevent it.
If in thy wisdom thou canst give no help,
Do thou but call my resolution wise
And with this knife I'll help it presently.
God joined my heart and Romeo's, thou our hands,
And ere this hand, by thee to Romeo's sealed,
Shall be the label to another deed, 57
Or my true heart with treacherous revolt
Turn to another, this shall slay them both.
Therefore, out of thy long-experienced time, 60
Give me some present counsel; or, behold
'Twixt my extremes and me this bloody knife 62
Shall play the umpire, arbitrating that
Which the commission of thy years and art 64
Could to no issue of true honor bring.
Be not so long to speak. I long to die
If what thou speak'st speak not of remedy.

FRIAR

Hold, daughter. I do spy a kind of hope,
Which craves as desperate an execution
As that is desperate which we would prevent.
If, rather than to marry County Paris, 70
Thou hast the strength of will to slay thyself,
Then it is likely thou wilt undertake
A thing like death to chide away this shame,
That cop'st with death himself to scape from it; 75
And, if thou darest, I'll give thee remedy.

JULIET

O, bid me leap, rather than marry Paris,

---

48 *prorogue* postpone 57 *label* i.e., strip of parchment bearing the seal, at-
tached to a deed 60 *time* age 62 *extremes* difficulties 64 *commission . . .
art* authority of your age and skill 75 *cop'st* encounterest

From off the battlements of any tower,
79 Or walk in thievish ways, or bid me lurk
80 Where serpents are, chain me with roaring bears,
81 Or hide me nightly in a charnel house,
O'ercovered quite with dead men's rattling bones,
83 With reeky shanks and yellow chapless skulls,
Or bid me go into a new-made grave
And hide me with a dead man in his shroud –
Things that, to hear them told, have made me tremble –
And I will do it without fear or doubt,
To live an unstained wife to my sweet love.

FRIAR
Hold, then. Go home, be merry, give consent
90 To marry Paris. Wednesday is tomorrow.
Tomorrow night look that thou lie alone;
Let not the nurse lie with thee in thy chamber.
Take thou this vial, being then in bed,
94 And this distilling liquor drink thou off;
When presently through all thy veins shall run
96 A cold and drowsy humor, for no pulse
97 Shall keep his native progress, but surcease,
No warmth, no breath, shall testify thou livest;
The roses in thy lips and cheeks shall fade
100 To wanny ashes, thy eyes' windows fall
Like death when he shuts up the day of life;
102 Each part, deprived of supple government,
Shall, stiff and stark and cold, appear like death;
And in this borrowed likeness of shrunk death
Thou shalt continue two-and-forty hours,
And then awake as from a pleasant sleep.
Now, when the bridegroom in the morning comes
To rouse thee from thy bed, there art thou dead.

---

79 *thievish ways* roads frequented by robbers   81 *charnel house* depository of
human bones   83 *reeky* smelly; *chapless* jawless   94 *distilling* infusing   96
humor moisture   97 *surcease* cease   100 *wanny* pale; *windows* i.e., eyelids
(the figure derives from the covering of shop fronts at the close of the day)
102 *supple government* the control of movement

Then, as the manner of our country is,
In thy best robes uncovered on the bier   *110*
Thou shalt be borne to that same ancient vault   111
Where all the kindred of the Capulets lie.
In the meantime, against thou shalt awake,   113
Shall Romeo by my letters know our drift,   114
And hither shall he come, and he and I
Will watch thy waking, and that very night
Shall Romeo bear thee hence to Mantua.
And this shall free thee from this present shame,
If no inconstant toy nor womanish fear   119
Abate thy valor in the acting it.   *120*

JULIET
Give me, give me! O, tell not me of fear!

FRIAR
Hold! Get you gone, be strong and prosperous
In this resolve. I'll send a friar with speed
To Mantua, with my letters to thy lord.

JULIET
Love give me strength! and strength shall help afford.
Farewell, dear father.   *Exit [with Friar].*

                            ✳

❧ **IV.2** *Enter [Capulet, his Wife], Nurse, and Serving-*
        men, two or three.

CAPULET
So many guests invite as here are writ.
                            [Exit a Servingman.]
Sirrah, go hire me twenty cunning cooks.

SERVINGMAN   You shall have none ill, sir, for I'll try if
they can lick their fingers.

---

111 (in Q2 this line is preceded by "Be borne to burial in thy kindred's
grave," evidently a canceled version of the line, printed in error) **113**
against . . . awake in preparation for your awaking **114** *drift* intention
119 *toy* whim
   IV.2 Capulet's house **s.d.** *two or three* (but only two are needed for the scene)

CAPULET

5   How canst thou try them so?

6 SERVINGMAN   Marry, sir, 'tis an ill cook that cannot lick
      his own fingers. Therefore he that cannot lick his fin-
      gers goes not with me.

CAPULET   Go, be gone.   *[Exit Servingman.]*

10   We shall be much unfurnished for this time.
      What, is my daughter gone to Friar Laurence?

NURSE   Ay, forsooth.

CAPULET
      Well, he may chance to do some good on her.

14   A peevish self-willed harlotry it is.
          Enter Juliet.

NURSE
      See where she comes from shrift with merry look.

CAPULET
      How now, my headstrong? Where have you been
         gadding?

JULIET
      Where I have learnt me to repent the sin
      Of disobedient opposition
      To you and your behests, and am enjoined

20   By holy Laurence to fall prostrate here
      To beg your pardon. Pardon, I beseech you!
      Henceforward I am ever ruled by you.

CAPULET
      Send for the county. Go tell him of this.

24   I'll have this knot knit up tomorrow morning.

JULIET
      I met the youthful lord at Laurence' cell
      And gave him what becomèd love I might,
      Not stepping o'er the bounds of modesty.

---

5 *try* test   6–7 *'tis . . . fingers* it's a poor cook who doesn't like to taste the
food which he prepares (proverbial)   10 *unfurnished* unprovided   14 *harlotry* hussy   24 *tomorrow morning* (i.e., Wednesday, one day earlier than
planned)

CAPULET
    Why, I am glad on't. This is well. Stand up.
    This is as't should be. Let me see the county.
    Ay, marry, go, I say, and fetch him hither.   *30*
    Now, afore God, this reverend holy friar,
    All our whole city is much bound to him.   *32*
JULIET
    Nurse, will you go with me into my closet
    To help me sort such needful ornaments
    As you think fit to furnish me tomorrow?
CAPULET'S WIFE
    No, not till Thursday. There is time enough.
CAPULET
    Go, nurse, go with her. We'll to church tomorrow.
                              Exeunt [Juliet and Nurse].
CAPULET'S WIFE
    We shall be short in our provision.
    'Tis now near night.
CAPULET   Tush, I will stir about,
    And all things shall be well, I warrant thee, wife.   *40*
    Go thou to Juliet, help to deck up her.
    I'll not to bed tonight; let me alone.
    I'll play the housewife for this once. What, ho!
    They are all forth; well, I will walk myself
    To County Paris, to prepare up him
    Against tomorrow. My heart is wondrous light,
    Since this same wayward girl is so reclaimed.
                                              [Exeunt.]

                              *

∾ IV.3 *Enter Juliet and Nurse.*

JULIET
    Ay, those attires are best, but, gentle nurse,

---

32 *bound* indebted
    IV.3 Juliet's chamber

I pray thee leave me to myself tonight,
3   For I have need of many orisons
To move the heavens to smile upon my state,
5   Which, well thou knowest, is cross and full of sin.
     Enter [Capulet's Wife].

CAPULET'S WIFE
   What, are you busy, ho? Need you my help?

JULIET
7   No, madam; we have culled such necessaries
8   As are behoveful for our state tomorrow.
So please you, let me now be left alone,
10   And let the nurse this night sit up with you,
For I am sure you have your hands full all
In this so sudden business.

CAPULET'S WIFE   Good night.
   Get thee to bed, and rest, for thou hast need.
         Exeunt [Capulet's Wife and Nurse].

JULIET
   Farewell! God knows when we shall meet again.
15   I have a faint cold fear thrills through my veins
That almost freezes up the heat of life.
I'll call them back again to comfort me.
Nurse! – What should she do here?
My dismal scene I needs must act alone.
20   Come, vial.
What if this mixture do not work at all?
Shall I be married then tomorrow morning?
No, no! This shall forbid it. Lie thou there.
     [Lays down a dagger.]
What if it be a poison which the friar
25   Subtly hath ministered to have me dead,
Lest in this marriage he should be dishonored
Because he married me before to Romeo?
I fear it is; and yet methinks it should not,

---

3 *orisons* prayers   5 *cross* perverse   7 *culled* picked out   8 *behoveful* fitting;
state ceremony   15 *faint* causing faintness   25 *ministered* administered

For he hath still been tried a holy man.   29
How if, when I am laid into the tomb,   30
I wake before the time that Romeo
Come to redeem me? There's a fearful point!
Shall I not then be stifled in the vault,
To whose foul mouth no healthsome air breathes in,
And there die strangled ere my Romeo comes?
Or, if I live, is it not very like
The horrible conceit of death and night,   37
Together with the terror of the place –
As in a vault, an ancient receptacle
Where for this many hundred years the bones   40
Of all my buried ancestors are packed,
Where bloody Tybalt, yet but green in earth,   42
Lies fest'ring in his shroud, where, as they say,
At some hours in the night spirits resort –
Alack, alack, is it not like that I,   45
So early waking – what with loathsome smells,
And shrieks like mandrakes torn out of the earth,   47
That living mortals, hearing them, run mad –
O, if I wake, shall I not be distraught,
Environèd with all these hideous fears,   50
And madly play with my forefathers' joints,
And pluck the mangled Tybalt from his shroud,
And, in this rage, with some great kinsman's bone
As with a club dash out my desp'rate brains?
O, look! methinks I see my cousin's ghost
Seeking out Romeo, that did spit his body
Upon a rapier's point. Stay, Tybalt, stay!

---

29 *tried* proved (after this line, Q1 inserts "I will not entertain so bad a thought") **37** *conceit* imagination **42** *green* new **45** *like* likely **47** *mandrakes* mandragora (a narcotic plant with a forked root resembling the human form, supposed to utter maddening shrieks when uprooted)

58   Romeo, Romeo, Romeo! Here's drink. I drink to thee.
      [She drinks from the vial and falls upon her bed
      within the curtains.]

                              *

～ **IV.4** *Enter [Capulet's Wife] and Nurse [with herbs].*

CAPULET'S WIFE
    Hold, take these keys and fetch more spices, nurse.
NURSE
    They call for dates and quinces in the pastry.
        Enter old Capulet.
CAPULET
    Come, stir, stir, stir! The second cock hath crowed,
    The curfew bell hath rung, 'tis three o'clock.
5   Look to the baked meats, good Angelica;
6   Spare not for cost.
NURSE   Go, you cot-quean, go,
    Get you to bed! Faith, you'll be sick tomorrow
8   For this night's watching.
CAPULET
    No, not a whit. What, I have watched ere now
10   All night for lesser cause, and ne'er been sick.
CAPULET'S WIFE
11   Ay, you have been a mouse-hunt in your time;
    But I will watch you from such watching now.
                            Exit [Capulet's Wife] and Nurse.

─────────

58 s.d. (Q1's s.d., "She falls upon her bed within the curtains," indicates that
Juliet's bed is visible onstage. It could be in the discovery space – in which
case the curtains would probably be the ones that hide the space – or could
have been thrust out onto the stage – when the curtains would be the bed
hangings.)
    IV.4 s.d. *with herbs* (from Q1)   **5** *baked meats* meat pies   **6** *cot-quean* a
man who plays housewife   **8** *watching* staying awake   **11** *mouse-hunt* i.e., a
nocturnal prowler after women

CAPULET

A jealous hood, a jealous hood!   13

Enter three or four [Fellows] with spits and logs and baskets.

                                Now, fellow,

What is there?

FIRST FELLOW

Things for the cook, sir, but I know not what.   15

CAPULET

Make haste, make haste.   *[Exit first Fellow.]*

                         Sirrah, fetch drier logs.

Call Peter; he will show thee where they are.

SECOND FELLOW

I have a head, sir, that will find out logs   18

And never trouble Peter for the matter.

CAPULET

Mass, and well said, a merry whoreson, ha!   20

Thou shalt be loggerhead.   21

                  [Exit second Fellow, with the others.]

                  Good faith, 'tis day.

The county will be here with music straight,

For so he said he would.

Play music [within].   I hear him near.

Nurse! Wife! What, ho! What, nurse, I say!

Enter Nurse.

Go waken Juliet; go and trim her up.   25

I'll go and chat with Paris. Hie, make haste,

Make haste! The bridegroom he is come already:

Make haste, I say.   *[Exit.]*

                         *

---

13 *A jealous hood* you wear the cap (or hood) of jealousy   15, 18 *First Fellow, Second Fellow* (Q2 reads "Fellow" in both instances)   18 *I . . . logs* i.e., my head is wooden and has an affinity for logs   20 *Mass* by the Mass; *whoreson* bastard, rascal   21 *loggerhead* blockhead   25 *trim her up* dress her neatly

✸ IV.5 *[Nurse goes to curtains.]*

NURSE
1   Mistress! what, mistress! Juliet! Fast, I warrant her, she.
2   Why, lamb! why, lady! Fie, you slugabed.
    Why, love, I say! madam! sweetheart! Why, bride!
4   What, not a word? You take your pennyworths now;
    Sleep for a week, for the next night, I warrant,
6   The County Paris hath set up his rest
    That you shall rest but little. God forgive me!
    Marry, and amen. How sound is she asleep!
    I needs must wake her. Madam, madam, madam!
10 Ay, let the county take you in your bed;
    He'll fright you up, i' faith. Will it not be?
        [Draws aside the curtains.]
12 What, dressed, and in your clothes, and down again?
    I must needs wake you. Lady! lady! lady!
    Alas, alas! Help, help! my lady's dead!
15 O welladay that ever I was born!
16 Some aqua vitae, ho! My lord! my lady!
        [Enter Capulet's Wife.]
CAPULET'S WIFE
    What noise is here?
NURSE   O lamentable day!
CAPULET'S WIFE
    What is the matter?
NURSE   Look, look! O heavy day!
CAPULET'S WIFE
    O me, O me! My child, my only life!
20 Revive, look up, or I will die with thee!
    Help, help! Call help.
        Enter Capulet.

IV.5 (The scene division is traditional but the action is continuous.) **1** *Fast*
fast asleep **2** *slugabed* sleepyhead **4** *pennyworths* small portions **6** *set . . .
rest* i.e., made his firm decision (from primero, a card game) **12** *down* back
to bed **15** *welladay* alas **16** *aqua vitae* alcoholic spirits

CAPULET

For shame, bring Juliet forth, her lord is come.

NURSE

She's dead, deceased, she's dead, alack the day!

CAPULET'S WIFE

Alack the day, she's dead, she's dead, she's dead!

CAPULET

Ha! let me see her. Out alas! she's cold,
Her blood is settled, and her joints are stiff;
Life and these lips have long been separated.
Death lies on her like an untimely frost
Upon the sweetest flower of all the field.

NURSE

O lamentable day!   30

CAPULET'S WIFE   O woeful time!

CAPULET

Death, that hath ta'en her hence to make me wail,
Ties up my tongue and will not let me speak.
      *Enter Friar [Laurence] and the County [Paris, with
      Musicians].*

FRIAR

Come, is the bride ready to go to church?

CAPULET

Ready to go, but never to return.
O son, the night before thy wedding day
Hath Death lain with thy wife. There she lies,
Flower as she was, deflowerèd by him.
Death is my son-in-law, Death is my heir;
My daughter he hath wedded. I will die
And leave him all. Life, living, all is Death's.   40
      [All at once cry out and wring their hands.]

PARIS

Have I thought long to see this morning's face,
And doth it give me such a sight as this?

───────

40 s.d. (from Q1; the s.d. suggests that the four mourners lament simulta-
neously, each having six lines of grief)

CAPULET'S WIFE
    Accursed, unhappy, wretched, hateful day!
    Most miserable hour that e'er time saw
45   In lasting labor of his pilgrimage!
46   But one, poor one, one poor and loving child,
    But one thing to rejoice and solace in,
    And cruel Death hath catched it from my sight.

NURSE
    O woe! O woeful, woeful, woeful day!
50   Most lamentable day, most woeful day
    That ever ever I did yet behold!
    O day, O day, O day! O hateful day!
    Never was seen so black a day as this.
    O woeful day! O woeful day!

PARIS
    Beguiled, divorcèd, wrongèd, spited, slain!
    Most detestable Death, by thee beguiled,
    By cruel cruel thee quite overthrown.
    O love! O life! not life, but love in death!

CAPULET
    Despised, distressèd, hated, martyred, killed!
60   Uncomfortable time, why cam'st thou now
61   To murder, murder our solemnity?
    O child, O child! my soul, and not my child!
    Dead art thou – alack, my child is dead,
    And with my child my joys are burièd!

FRIAR
    Peace, ho, for shame! Confusion's cure lives not
    In these confusions. Heaven and yourself
    Had part in this fair maid – now heaven hath all,
    And all the better is it for the maid.
69   Your part in her you could not keep from death,

---

45 *lasting labor* continuous toil 46 *But one* (cf. III.5.166) 61 *To murder . . . solemnity* to spoil our ceremony 69 *Your part* her mortal body, generated by her parents

But heaven keeps his part in eternal life.   70
The most you sought was her promotion,
For 'twas your heaven she should be advanced;
And weep ye now, seeing she is advanced
Above the clouds, as high as heaven itself?
O, in this love, you love your child so ill
That you run mad, seeing that she is well.
She's not well married that lives married long,
But she's best married that dies married young.
Dry up your tears and stick your rosemary   79
On this fair corpse, and, as the custom is,   80
In all her best array bear her to church;
For though fond nature bids us all lament,   82
Yet nature's tears are reason's merriment.   83

CAPULET
All things that we ordainèd festival
Turn from their office to black funeral –
Our instruments to melancholy bells,
Our wedding cheer to a sad burial feast,
Our solemn hymns to sullen dirges change,
Our bridal flowers serve for a buried corpse,
And all things change them to the contrary.   90

FRIAR
Sir, go you in, and, madam, go with him,
And go, Sir Paris. Everyone prepare
To follow this fair corpse unto her grave.
The heavens do low'r upon you for some ill;   94
Move them no more by crossing their high will.   95

        Exeunt [casting rosemary on her and shutting the
              curtains]. Manet [the Nurse with Musicians].

FIRST MUSICIAN
Faith, we may put up our pipes and be gone.

----

70 *his part* her immortal soul, created directly by God   79 *rosemary* plant symbolizing remembrance   82 *fond nature* foolish human nature   83 *merriment* cause for optimism   94 *low'r* look angrily; *ill* sin   95 s.d. *casting . . . curtains* (from Q1)

NURSE

> Honest good fellows, ah, put up, put up!
>
> 98 For well you know this is a pitiful case.   *[Exit.]*

FIRST MUSICIAN

> 99 Ay, by my troth, the case may be amended.

> *Enter Peter.*

100 PETER   Musicians, O, musicians, "Heart's ease," "Heart's ease"! O, an you will have me live, play "Heart's ease."

FIRST MUSICIAN   Why "Heart's ease"?

103 PETER   O, musicians, because my heart itself plays "My
104 heart is full of woe." O, play me some merry dump to comfort me.

FIRST MUSICIAN   Not a dump we! 'Tis no time to play now.

PETER   You will not then?

FIRST MUSICIAN   No.

PETER   I will then give it you soundly.

110 FIRST MUSICIAN   What will you give us?

111 PETER   No money, on my faith, but the gleek. I will give you the minstrel.

FIRST MUSICIAN   Then will I give you the serving-creature.

PETER   Then will I lay the serving-creature's dagger on
115 your pate. I will carry no crotchets. I'll re you, I'll fa you. Do you note me?

FIRST MUSICIAN   An you re us and fa us, you note us.

SECOND MUSICIAN   Pray you put up your dagger, and
119 put out your wit.

120 PETER   Then have at you with my wit! I will dry-beat you with an iron wit, and put up my iron dagger. Answer me like men.

---

98 s.d. (Q2 reads "Exit omnes.") 99 *the case . . . amended* (1) things could be better, (2) the instrument case could be repaired; s.d. *Enter Peter* (Q2 has "Enter Will Kemp," the famous comic actor playing Peter's role) 100, 103–4 *Heart's ease; My heart is full of woe* (old ballad tunes) 104 *dump* mournful dance tune 111 *gleek* mock 111–12 *give you* insultingly call you 115 *carry* put up with; *crotchets* (1) whims, (2) quarter notes in music; *re, fa* (musical notes) 119 *put out* display 120 *Then . . . wit* (added to preceding speech in Q2); *dry-beat* thrash

"When griping grief the heart doth wound,   123
    And doleful dumps the mind oppress,
  Then music with her silver sound" –
Why "silver sound"? Why "music with her silver
sound"? What say you, Simon Catling?   127

FIRST MUSICIAN Marry, sir, because silver hath a sweet
sound.

PETER Pretty! What say you, Hugh Rebeck?   130

SECOND MUSICIAN I say "silver sound" because musicians
sound for silver.

PETER Pretty too! What say you, James Soundpost?   133

THIRD MUSICIAN Faith, I know not what to say.

PETER O, I cry you mercy! you are the singer. I will say   135
for you. It is "music with her silver sound" because musicians have no gold for sounding.
    "Then music with her silver sound
      With speedy help doth lend redress."   *Exit.*

FIRST MUSICIAN What a pestilent knave is this same!   140

SECOND MUSICIAN Hang him, Jack! Come, we'll in here,
tarry for the mourners, and stay dinner.   142
                      Exit [with others].

                  ✻

❧ **V.1** *Enter Romeo*

ROMEO
If I may trust the flattering truth of sleep,   1
My dreams presage some joyful news at hand.
My bosom's lord sits lightly in his throne,   3
And all this day an unaccustomed spirit

123–25 (The second line is missing in Q2 but appears in Q1. The song is
from Richard Edwards's "In Commendation of Music," in *The Paradise of
Dainty Devices,* 1576.) 127 *Catling* (lutestring) 130 *Rebeck* (three-
stringed fiddle) 133 *Soundpost* (wooden peg in a violin, supporting the
bridge) 135 *cry you mercy* beg your pardon 142 *stay* await
  V.1 Mantua 1 *flattering* favorable to me; *truth of sleep* (cf. I.4.52)
3 *bosom's lord* heart

Lifts me above the ground with cheerful thoughts.
I dreamt my lady came and found me dead
(Strange dream that gives a dead man leave to think!)
And breathed such life with kisses in my lips
That I revived and was an emperor.

10 Ah me! how sweet is love itself possessed,
11 When but love's shadows are so rich in joy!
    Enter Romeo's man [Balthasar, booted].
News from Verona! How now, Balthasar?
Dost thou not bring me letters from the friar?
How doth my lady? Is my father well?
How fares my Juliet? That I ask again,
For nothing can be ill if she be well.

BALTHASAR
Then she is well, and nothing can be ill.
Her body sleeps in Capel's monument,
And her immortal part with angels lives.
20 I saw her laid low in her kindred's vault
21 And presently took post to tell it you.
O, pardon me for bringing these ill news,
Since you did leave it for my office, sir.

ROMEO
24 Is it e'en so? Then I defy you, stars!
Thou knowest my lodging. Get me ink and paper
And hire post-horses. I will hence tonight.

BALTHASAR
I do beseech you, sir, have patience.
28 Your looks are pale and wild and do import
Some misadventure.

ROMEO   Tush, thou art deceived.
30 Leave me and do the thing I bid thee do.
Hast thou no letters to me from the friar?

BALTHASAR
No, my good lord.

---

11 *shadows* dream images **11 s.d.** *booted* (from Q1) **21** *presently* at once;
took post hired post-horses **24** *stars* (cf. I.4.107) **28** *import* suggest

ROMEO   No matter. Get thee gone
  And hire those horses. I'll be with thee straight.
                                Exit [Balthasar].
  Well, Juliet, I will lie with thee tonight.
  Let's see for means. O mischief, thou art swift
  To enter in the thoughts of desperate men!
  I do remember an apothecary,
  And hereabouts a dwells, which late I noted
  In tattered weeds, with overwhelming brows,   39
  Culling of simples. Meager were his looks,   40
  Sharp misery had worn him to the bones,
  And in his needy shop a tortoise hung,
  An alligator stuffed, and other skins
  Of ill-shaped fishes, and about his shelves
  A beggarly account of empty boxes,   45
  Green earthen pots, bladders, and musty seeds,
  Remnants of packthread, and old cakes of roses   47
  Were thinly scattered, to make up a show.
  Noting this penury, to myself I said,
  "An if a man did need a poison now   50
  Whose sale is present death in Mantua,
  Here lives a caitiff wretch would sell it him."   52
  O, this same thought did but forerun my need,
  And this same needy man must sell it me.
  As I remember, this should be the house.
  Being holiday, the beggar's shop is shut.
  What, ho! apothecary!
    [Enter Apothecary.]
APOTHECARY   Who calls so loud?
ROMEO
  Come hither, man. I see that thou art poor.
  Hold, there is forty ducats. Let me have
  A dram of poison, such soon-speeding gear   60

---

39 *weeds* garments; *overwhelming* overhanging **40** *simples* herbs **45** *account* quantity **47** *cakes of roses* compressed rose petals, used for perfume
52 *caitiff* miserable **60** *gear* stuff

As will disperse itself through all the veins
That the life-weary taker may fall dead,
And that the trunk may be discharged of breath
As violently as hasty powder fired
65   Doth hurry from the fatal cannon's womb.
APOTHECARY
66   Such mortal drugs I have; but Mantua's law
67   Is death to any he that utters them.
ROMEO
Art thou so bare and full of wretchedness
And fearest to die? Famine is in thy cheeks,
70   Need and oppression starveth in thy eyes,
Contempt and beggary hangs upon thy back.
The world is not thy friend, nor the world's law.
The world affords no law to make thee rich;
Then be not poor, but break it and take this.
APOTHECARY
My poverty but not my will consents.
ROMEO
I pay thy poverty and not thy will.
APOTHECARY
Put this in any liquid thing you will
And drink it off, and if you had the strength
Of twenty men, it would dispatch you straight.
ROMEO
80   There is thy gold – worse poison to men's souls,
Doing more murder in this loathsome world,
Than these poor compounds that thou mayst not sell.
I sell thee poison; thou hast sold me none.
Farewell. Buy food and get thyself in flesh.
Come, cordial and not poison, go with me
To Juliet's grave, for there must I use thee.   *Exeunt.*

*

---

65 *womb* i.e., barrel **66** *mortal* deadly **67** *utters* gives out **70** *starveth* are revealed by the starved look

∞ **V.2** *Enter Friar John to Friar Laurence.*

FRIAR JOHN
  Holy Franciscan friar, brother, ho!
    Enter [Friar] Laurence.
FRIAR LAURENCE
  This same should be the voice of Friar John.
  Welcome from Mantua. What says Romeo?
  Or, if his mind be writ, give me his letter.
FRIAR JOHN
  Going to find a barefoot brother out,   5
  One of our order, to associate me   6
  Here in this city visiting the sick,
  And finding him, the searchers of the town,   8
  Suspecting that we both were in a house
  Where the infectious pestilence did reign,   10
  Sealed up the doors, and would not let us forth,
  So that my speed to Mantua there was stayed.
FRIAR LAURENCE
  Who bare my letter, then, to Romeo?
FRIAR JOHN
  I could not send it – here it is again –
  Nor get a messenger to bring it thee,
  So fearful were they of infection.
FRIAR LAURENCE
  Unhappy fortune! By my brotherhood,   17
  The letter was not nice, but full of charge,   18
  Of dear import; and the neglecting it
  May do much danger. Friar John, go hence,   20
  Get me an iron crow and bring it straight   21
  Unto my cell.

V.2 Friar Laurence's cell 5 *a barefoot brother* another friar 6 *associate* accompany 8 *searchers* health officers 10 *pestilence* plague 17 *brotherhood*
order (Franciscans) 18 *nice* trivial; *charge* important matters 21 *crow*
crowbar

FRIAR JOHN   Brother, I'll go and bring it thee.   *Exit.*
FRIAR LAURENCE
       Now must I to the monument alone.
       Within this three hours will fair Juliet wake.
25   She will beshrew me much that Romeo
26   Hath had no notice of these accidents;
       But I will write again to Mantua,
       And keep her at my cell till Romeo come –
       Poor living corpse, closed in a dead man's tomb!   *Exit.*

                              ✳

   ❧ **V.3** *Enter Paris and his Page [with flowers and sweet
       water and a torch].*

PARIS
       Give me thy torch, boy. Hence, and stand aloof.
       Yet put it out, for I would not be seen.
3   Under yond yew tree lay thee all along,
       Holding thy ear close to the hollow ground.
       So shall no foot upon the churchyard tread
       (Being loose, unfirm, with digging up of graves)
       But thou shalt hear it. Whistle then to me,
       As signal that thou hearest something approach.
       Give me those flowers. Do as I bid thee, go.
   PAGE   *[Aside]*
10   I am almost afraid to stand alone
11   Here in the churchyard; yet I will adventure.
           [Retires. Paris strews the tomb with flowers.]
   PARIS
       Sweet flower, with flowers thy bridal bed I strew
           (O woe! thy canopy is dust and stones)
       Which with sweet water nightly I will dew;
           Or, wanting that, with tears distilled by moans.

---

25 *beshrew* reprove   26 *accidents* occurrences
      V.3 Verona   **s.d.** *with . . . water* (from Q1); *sweet* perfumed   **3** *all along*
at full length   **11 s.d.** *Paris . . . flowers* (from Q1)

The obsequies that I for thee will keep
Nightly shall be to strew thy grave and weep.
    Whistle Boy.
The boy gives warning something doth approach.
What cursèd foot wanders this way tonight
To cross my obsequies and true love's rite?   20
What, with a torch? Muffle me, night, awhile. *[Retires.]*   21
    Enter Romeo [and Balthasar with a torch, a mattock,
    and a crow of iron].

ROMEO
Give me that mattock and the wrenching iron.
Hold, take this letter. Early in the morning
See thou deliver it to my lord and father.
Give me the light. Upon thy life I charge thee,
Whate'er thou hearest or seest, stand all aloof
And do not interrupt me in my course.
Why I descend into this bed of death
Is partly to behold my lady's face,
But chiefly to take thence from her dead finger   30
A precious ring – a ring that I must use   31
In dear employment. Therefore hence, be gone.
But if thou, jealous, dost return to pry   33
In what I farther shall intend to do,
By heaven, I will tear thee joint by joint
And strew this hungry churchyard with thy limbs.
The time and my intents are savage-wild,
More fierce and more inexorable far
Than empty tigers or the roaring sea.

BALTHASAR
I will be gone, sir, and not trouble you.   40

ROMEO
So shalt thou show me friendship. Take thou that.

---

20 *cross* interfere with   **21 s.d.** *and Balthasar . . . iron* (from Q1; Q2 reads
"Enter Romeo and Peter" and gives the speech prefix "Peter" at ll. 40 and
43); *mattock* pickax   **31** *A precious ring* (a false excuse to assure Balthasar's
noninterference)   **33** *jealous* curious

[Gives him money.]
Live, and be prosperous; and farewell, good fellow.
BALTHASAR   *[Aside]*
    For all this same, I'll hide me hereabout.
    His looks I fear, and his intents I doubt. *[Retires.]*
ROMEO
    Thou detestable maw, thou womb of death,
    Gorged with the dearest morsel of the earth,
    Thus I enforce thy rotten jaws to open,
48   And in despite I'll cram thee with more food.
    [Romeo begins to open the tomb.]

PARIS
    This is that banished haughty Montague
50   That murdered my love's cousin – with which grief
    It is supposèd the fair creature died –
    And here is come to do some villainous shame
53   To the dead bodies. I will apprehend him.
    Stop thy unhallowed toil, vile Montague!
    Can vengeance be pursued further than death?
    Condemnèd villain, I do apprehend thee.
    Obey, and go with me, for thou must die.
ROMEO
    I must indeed, and therefore came I hither.
    Good gentle youth, tempt not a desp'rate man.
60   Fly hence and leave me. Think upon these gone;
    Let them affright thee. I beseech thee, youth,
    Put not another sin upon my head
    By urging me to fury. O, be gone!
    By heaven, I love thee better than myself,
    For I come hither armed against myself.
    Stay not, be gone. Live, and hereafter say
    A madman's mercy bid thee run away.

---

48 *in despite* to spite you; **s.d.** (From Q1, "Romeo opens the tomb.") **53** *apprehend* arrest   **60** *gone* dead

PARIS

   I do defy thy conjurations   68

   And apprehend thee for a felon here.

ROMEO

   Wilt thou provoke me? Then have at thee, boy!   70

    [They fight.]

PAGE

   O Lord, they fight! I will go call the watch.

                         [Exit. Paris falls.]

PARIS

   O, I am slain! If thou be merciful,

   Open the tomb, lay me with Juliet.   *[Dies.]*

ROMEO

   In faith, I will. Let me peruse this face.   74

   Mercutio's kinsman, noble County Paris!

   What said my man when my betossèd soul

   Did not attend him as we rode? I think   77

   He told me Paris should have married Juliet.

   Said he not so? or did I dream it so?

   Or am I mad, hearing him talk of Juliet,   80

   To think it was so? O, give me thy hand,

   One writ with me in sour misfortune's book!

   I'll bury thee in a triumphant grave.   83

    [Romeo opens the tomb.]

   A grave? O, no, a lantern, slaughtered youth,   84

   For here lies Juliet, and her beauty makes

   This vault a feasting presence full of light.   86

   Death, lie thou there, by a dead man interred.

    [Lays him in the tomb.]

   How oft when men are at the point of death

   Have they been merry! which their keepers call   89

---

68 *conjurations* threatening appeals   **74** *peruse* read, look at   **77** *attend* pay attention to   **83 s.d.** (Juliet is now visible, probably still lying on the bed from IV.5, which has now become her tomb)   **84** *lantern* a many-windowed turret room   **86** *presence* presence chamber   **89** *keepers* jailers

90 A lightening before death. O, how may I
    Call this a lightening? O my love! my wife!
    Death, that hath sucked the honey of thy breath,
    Hath had no power yet upon thy beauty.
94 Thou are not conquered. Beauty's ensign yet
    Is crimson in thy lips and in thy cheeks,
    And death's pale flag is not advancèd there.
    Tybalt, liest thou there in thy bloody sheet?
    O, what more favor can I do to thee
    Than with that hand that cut thy youth in twain
100 To sunder his that was thine enemy?
    Forgive me, cousin! Ah, dear Juliet,
102 Why art thou yet so fair? Shall I believe
    That unsubstantial Death is amorous,
    And that the lean abhorrèd monster keeps
    Thee here in dark to be his paramour?
    For fear of that I still will stay with thee
    And never from this pallet of dim night
108 Depart again. Here, here will I remain
    With worms that are thy chambermaids. O, here
110 Will I set up my everlasting rest
111 And shake the yoke of inauspicious stars
    From this world-wearied flesh. Eyes, look your last!
    Arms, take your last embrace! and, lips, O you
    The doors of breath, seal with a righteous kiss
115 A dateless bargain to engrossing death!
116 Come, bitter conduct; come, unsavory guide!
117 Thou desperate pilot, now at once run on

---

94 *ensign* banner **102** *Why . . . fair* (followed in Q2 by a superfluous "I will believe," evidently another manuscript cancelation printed in error) **108** *again. Here* (Q2 prints between these words the following material, obviously canceled in the manuscript because it appears in substance later in the speech: "come lie thou in my arm / Here's to thy health, where e'er thou tumblest in / O true Apothecary! / Thy drugs are quick. Thus with a kiss I die. / Depart again.") **110** *set . . . rest* make my decision to stay forever (cf. IV.5.6) **111** *inauspicious stars* (cf. V.1.24) **115** *dateless* in perpetuity; *engrossing* taking everything **116** *conduct* guide – i.e., the poison **117** *pilot* i.e., Romeo's soul

The dashing rocks thy seasick weary bark!   118
Here's to my love! *[Drinks.]* O true apothecary!   119
Thy drugs are quick. Thus with a kiss I die.   *120*
   [He kisses Juliet, falls, and dies.]
   Enter Friar [Laurence], with lantern, crow, and spade.
FRIAR
Saint Francis be my speed! how oft tonight   121
Have my old feet stumbled at graves! Who's there?   122
BALTHASAR
Here's one, a friend, and one that knows you well.
FRIAR
Bliss be upon you! Tell me, good my friend,
What torch is yond that vainly lends his light
To grubs and eyeless skulls? As I discern,
It burneth in the Capels' monument.
BALTHASAR
It doth so, holy sir; and there's my master,
One that you love.
FRIAR   Who is it?
BALTHASAR   Romeo.
FRIAR
How long hath he been there?   *130*
BALTHASAR   Full half an hour.
FRIAR
Go with me to the vault.
BALTHASAR   I dare not, sir.
My master knows not but I am gone hence,
And fearfully did menace me with death
If I did stay to look on his intents.
FRIAR
Stay then; I'll go alone. Fear comes upon me.
O, much I fear some ill unthrifty thing.   136
BALTHASAR
As I did sleep under this yew tree here,

---

118 *bark* i.e., Romeo's body   119 *Here's to my love* (cf. IV.3.58)   121 *speed* aid   122 *stumbled at graves* (a bad omen)   136 *unthrifty* unfortunate

I dreamt my master and another fought,
139 And that my master slew him.
FRIAR   Romeo!
    [Friar stoops and looks on the blood and weapons.]
140 Alack, alack, what blood is this which stains
    The stony entrance of this sepulcher?
    What mean these masterless and gory swords
    To lie discolored by this place of peace?
        [Enters the tomb.]
    Romeo! O, pale! Who else? What, Paris too?
    And steeped in blood? Ah, what an unkind hour
    Is guilty of this lamentable chance!
    The lady stirs.
        [Juliet rises.]
JULIET
148 O comfortable friar! where is my lord?
    I do remember well where I should be,
150 And there I am. Where is my Romeo?
FRIAR
    I hear some noise. Lady, come from that nest
    Of death, contagion, and unnatural sleep.
    A greater power than we can contradict
    Hath thwarted our intents. Come, come away.
    Thy husband in thy bosom there lies dead;
    And Paris too. Come, I'll dispose of thee
    Among a sisterhood of holy nuns.
    Stay not to question, for the watch is coming.
    Come, go, good Juliet. I dare no longer stay.
JULIET
160 Go, get thee hence, for I will not away.   *Exit [Friar].*
    What's here? A cup, closed in my true love's hand?
162 Poison, I see, hath been his timeless end.
    O churl! drunk all, and left no friendly drop

---

139 s.d. (from Q1)   **147 s.d.** (from Q1) **148** *comfortable* comfort-giving
162 *timeless* untimely

To help me after? I will kiss thy lips.
Haply some poison yet doth hang on them   166
To make me die with a restorative.
   [Kisses him.]
Thy lips are warm!

CHIEF WATCHMAN   *[Within]* Lead, boy. Which way?

JULIET   169
Yea, noise? Then I'll be brief. O happy dagger!
   [Takes Romeo's dagger.]   170
This is thy sheath; there rust, and let me die.
   [She stabs herself, falls, and dies.]
   Enter [Paris's Page] and Watch.

PAGE
This is the place. There, where the torch doth burn.

CHIEF WATCHMAN
The ground is bloody. Search about the churchyard.   173
Go, some of you; whoe'er you find attach.
                              [Exeunt some of the Watch.]
Pitiful sight! here lies the county slain;
And Juliet bleeding, warm, and newly dead,
Who here hath lain this two days burièd.
Go, tell the prince; run to the Capulets;
Raise up the Montagues; some others search.
                              [Exeunt others of the Watch.]
We see the ground whereon these woes do lie,   180
But the true ground of all these piteous woes   181
We cannot without circumstance descry.
   Enter [some of the Watch, with] Romeo's Man
   [Balthasar].

SECOND WATCHMAN
Here's Romeo's man. We found him in the churchyard.

CHIEF WATCHMAN
Hold him in safety till the prince come hither.

---

166 *restorative* i.e., restoring me to you   169 *happy* opportune   170 *rust*
(Q1 "rest")   173 *attach* arrest   180 *ground* basis   181 *circumstance* details

Enter Friar [Laurence] and another Watchman.

THIRD WATCHMAN
 Here is a friar that trembles, sighs, and weeps.
 We took this mattock and this spade from him
 As he was coming from this churchyard side.

CHIEF WATCHMAN
 A great suspicion! Stay the friar too.
  Enter the Prince [and Attendants].

PRINCE
 What misadventure is so early up,
189 That calls our person from our morning rest?
  Enter Capulet and his Wife.

CAPULET
190 What should it be, that is so shrieked abroad?

CAPULET'S WIFE
 O, the people in the street cry "Romeo,"
 Some "Juliet," and some "Paris"; and all run,
 With open outcry, toward our monument.

PRINCE
 What fear is this which startles in your ears?

CHIEF WATCHMAN
 Sovereign, here lies the County Paris slain;
 And Romeo dead; and Juliet, dead before,
 Warm and new killed.

PRINCE
 Search, seek, and know how this foul murder comes.

CHIEF WATCHMAN
 Here is a friar, and slaughtered Romeo's man,
200 With instruments upon them fit to open
201 These dead men's tombs.

CAPULET
 O heavens! O wife, look how our daughter bleeds!

---

189 s.d. *Enter . . . Wife* (in Q2 "Enter Capels" appears here, with the present
stage direction after l. 201; "Capels" might mean that other Capulets are
with them) **201** (Q2's s.d., after this line, for Capulet and his wife to enter
at this point may mean they enter the tomb)

This dagger hath mista'en, for, lo, his house   203
Is empty on the back of Montague,
And it missheathèd in my daughter's bosom!

CAPULET'S WIFE
O me! this sight of death is as a bell
That warns my old age to a sepulcher.   207
    Enter Montague.

PRINCE
Come, Montague, for thou art early up
To see thy son and heir more early down.

MONTAGUE
Alas, my liege, my wife is dead tonight!   *210*
Grief of my son's exile hath stopped her breath.
What further woe conspires against mine age?

PRINCE
Look, and thou shalt see.

MONTAGUE   *[To Romeo's corpse]*
O thou untaught! what manners is in this,
To press before thy father to a grave?

PRINCE
Seal up the mouth of outrage for a while,   216
Till we can clear these ambiguities
And know their spring, their head, their true descent;
And then will I be general of your woes   219
And lead you even to death. Meantime forbear,   220
And let mischance be slave to patience.
Bring forth the parties of suspicion.

FRIAR
I am the greatest, able to do least,
Yet most suspected, as the time and place
Doth make against me, of this direful murder;

---

203 *his house* its sheath   **207** *my old age* (though she may be only twenty-eight [I.3.72–73], she feels old and ready for death; cf. III.2.89); **s.d.** (Montague may enter with other Montagues)   **216** *mouth of outrage* violent outcries   **219** *general . . . woes* your leader in lamentation   **220** *even to death* even if grief kills us

226 And here I stand, both to impeach and purge
    Myself condemnèd and myself excused.

PRINCE
    Then say at once what thou dost know in this.

FRIAR
229 I will be brief, for my short date of breath
230 Is not so long as is a tedious tale.
    Romeo, there dead, was husband to that Juliet;
    And she, there dead, that Romeo's faithful wife.
    I married them, and their stol'n marriage day
    Was Tybalt's doomsday, whose untimely death
    Banished the new-made bridegroom from this city;
    For whom, and not for Tybalt, Juliet pined.
    You, to remove that siege of grief from her,
238 Betrothed and would have married her perforce
    To County Paris. Then comes she to me
240 And with wild looks bid me devise some mean
    To rid her from this second marriage,
    Or in my cell there would she kill herself.
    Then gave I her (so tutored by my art)
    A sleeping potion, which so took effect
    As I intended, for it wrought on her
    The form of death. Meantime I writ to Romeo
247 That he should hither come as this dire night
    To help to take her from her borrowed grave,
    Being the time the potion's force should cease.
250 But he which bore my letter, Friar John,
    Was stayed by accident, and yesternight
    Returned my letter back. Then all alone
    At the prefixèd hour of her waking
    Came I to take her from her kindred's vault,
255 Meaning to keep her closely at my cell
    Till I conveniently could send to Romeo.
    But when I came, some minute ere the time

---

226 *impeach and purge* accuse and exonerate 229 *date of breath* life expectancy 238 *perforce* by force 247 *as* on 255 *closely* secretly

Of her awakening, here untimely lay
The noble Paris and true Romeo dead.
She wakes, and I entreated her come forth   260
And bear this work of heaven with patience.
But then a noise did scare me from the tomb,
And she, too desperate, would not go with me,
But, as it seems, did violence on herself.
All this I know, and to the marriage
Her nurse is privy, and if aught in this   266
Miscarried by my fault, let my old life
Be sacrificed, some hour before his time,
Unto the rigor of severest law.

PRINCE
We still have known thee for a holy man.   270
Where's Romeo's man? What can he say in this?

BALTHASAR
I brought my master news of Juliet's death;
And then in post he came from Mantua
To this same place, to this same monument.
This letter he early bid me give his father,
And threatened me with death, going in the vault,
If I departed not and left him there.

PRINCE
Give me the letter. I will look on it.
Where is the county's page that raised the watch?
Sirrah, what made your master in this place?   280

PAGE
He came with flowers to strew his lady's grave,
And bid me stand aloof, and so I did.
Anon comes one with light to ope the tomb,   283
And by and by my master drew on him,   284
And then I ran away to call the watch.

PRINCE
This letter doth make good the friar's words,

---

266 *privy* in on the secret   **270** *still* always   **280** *made* did   **283** *Anon* soon
284 *by and by* almost at once; *drew* drew his sword

Their course of love, the tidings of her death,
And here he writes that he did buy a poison
Of a poor pothecary, and therewithal
290 Came to this vault to die, and lie with Juliet.
Where be these enemies? Capulet, Montague,
See what a scourge is laid upon your hate,
293 That heaven finds means to kill your joys with love.
294 And I, for winking at your discords too,
295 Have lost a brace of kinsmen. All are punished.
CAPULET
O brother Montague, give me thy hand.
297 This is my daughter's jointure, for no more
Can I demand.
MONTAGUE   But I can give thee more;
For I will raise her statue in pure gold,
300 That whiles Verona by that name is known,
301 There shall no figure at such rate be set
As that of true and faithful Juliet.
CAPULET
As rich shall Romeo's by his lady's lie –
Poor sacrifices of our enmity!
PRINCE
305 A glooming peace this morning with it brings.
The sun for sorrow will not show his head.
Go hence, to have more talk of these sad things;
Some shall be pardoned, and some punishèd;
For never was a story of more woe
310 Than this of Juliet and her Romeo.   *[Exeunt omnes.]*

---

293 *joys* happiness, children; *with* by means of   **294** *winking at* shutting my
eyes to   **295** *brace* pair (Mercutio and Paris)   **297** *jointure* marriage portion
301 *rate* value   **305** *glooming* cloudy, overcast

NOW AVAILABLE

Antony and Cleopatra
ISBN 0-14-071452-9

The Comedy of Errors
ISBN 0-14-071474-X

Coriolanus
ISBN 0-14-071473-1

Cymbeline
ISBN 0-14-071472-3

Henry IV, Part I
ISBN 0-14-071456-1

Henry IV, Part 2
ISBN 0-14-071457-X

Henry V
ISBN 0-14-071458-8

King Lear
ISBN 0-14-071476-6

King Lear (The Quarto and Folio Texts)
ISBN 0-14-071490-1

Macbeth
ISBN 0-14-071478-2

Much Ado About Nothing
ISBN 0-14-071480-4

The Narrative Poems
ISBN 0-14-071481-2

Richard III
ISBN 0-14-071483-9

Romeo and Juliet
ISBN 0-14-071484-7

The Tempest
ISBN 0-14-071485-5

Timon of Athens
ISBN 0-14-071487-1

Titus Andronicus
ISBN 0-14-071491-X

Twelfth Night
ISBN 0-14-071489-8

The Two Gentlemen of Verona
ISBN 0-14-071461-8

The Winter's Tale
ISBN 0-14-071488-X

FORTHCOMING

All's Well That Ends Well
ISBN 0-14-071460-X

As You Like It
ISBN 0-14-071471-5

Hamlet
ISBN 0-14-071454-5

Henry VI, Part 1
ISBN 0-14-071465-0

Henry VI, Part 2
ISBN 0-14-071466-9

Henry VI, Part 3
ISBN 0-14-071467-7

Henry VIII
ISBN 0-14-071475-8

Julius Caesar
ISBN 0-14-071468-5

King John
ISBN 0-14-071459-6

Love's Labor's Lost
ISBN 0-14-071477-4

Measure for Measure
ISBN 0-14-071479-0

The Merchant of Venice
ISBN 0-14-071462-6

The Merry Wives of Windsor
ISBN 0-14-071464-2

A Midsummer Night's Dream
ISBN 0-14-071455-3

Othello
ISBN 0-14-071463-4

Pericles
ISBN 0-14-071469-3

Richard II
ISBN 0-14-071482-0

The Sonnets
ISBN 0-14-071453-7

The Taming of the Shrew
ISBN 0-14-071451-0

Troilus and Cressida
ISBN 0-14-071486-3

FOR THE BEST IN PAPERBACKS, LOOK FOR THE

In every corner of the world, on every subject under the sun, Penguin represents quality and variety—the very best in publishing today.

For complete information about books available from Penguin—including Puffins, Penguin Classics, and Arkana—and how to order them, write to us at the appropriate address below. Please note that for copyright reasons the selection of books varies from country to country.

In the United Kingdom: Please write to *Dept. EP, Penguin Books Ltd, Bath Road, Harmondsworth, West Drayton, Middlesex UB7 0DA.*

In the United States: Please write to *Penguin Putnam Inc., P.O. Box 12289 Dept. B, Newark, New Jersey 07101-5289* or call 1-800-788-6262.

In Canada: Please write to *Penguin Books Canada Ltd, 10 Alcorn Avenue, Suite 300, Toronto, Ontario M4V 3B2.*

In Australia: Please write to *Penguin Books Australia Ltd, P.O. Box 257, Ringwood, Victoria 3134.*

In New Zealand: Please write to *Penguin Books (NZ) Ltd, Private Bag 102902, North Shore Mail Centre, Auckland 10.*

In India: Please write to *Penguin Books India Pvt Ltd, 11 Panchsheel Shopping Centre, Panchsheel Park, New Delhi 110 017.*

In the Netherlands: Please write to *Penguin Books Netherlands bv, Postbus 3507, NL-1001 AH Amsterdam.*

In Germany: Please write to *Penguin Books Deutschland GmbH, Metzlerstrasse 26, 60594 Frankfurt am Main.*

In Spain: Please write to *Penguin Books S. A., Bravo Murillo 19, 1° B, 28015 Madrid.*

In Italy: Please write to *Penguin Italia s.r.l., Via Benedetto Croce 2, 20094 Corsico, Milano.*

In France: Please write to *Penguin France, Le Carré Wilson, 62 rue Benjamin Baillaud, 31500 Toulouse.*

In Japan: Please write to *Penguin Books Japan Ltd, Kaneko Building, 2-3-25 Koraku, Bunkyo-Ku, Tokyo 112.*

In South Africa: Please write to *Penguin Books South Africa (Pty) Ltd, Private Bag X14, Parkview, 2122 Johannesburg.*